SAWTOOTH

Steph Nelson

CEMETERY GATES
MEDIA

Sawtooth
Published by Cemetery Gates Media
Binghamton, New York

Copyright © 2023
By Steph Nelson

All rights reserved. Without limiting the rights under the copyright reserved above, no part of this publication may be reproduced, stored in, or introduced into a retrieval system, or transmitted in any form or by any means (electronic, mechanical, photocopying, recording, or otherwise) without prior written permission.

ISBN: 9798861102674

For more information about this book and other Cemetery Gates Media publications, visit us at:

cemeterygatesmedia.com
twitter.com/cemeterygatesm
instagram.com/cemeterygatesm

Cover Art and Design: Carrion House

For Chris Nelson

PRAISE FOR STEPH NELSON

"Once *Sawtooth* sinks its teeth into you, it won't let go until the last page. This survival horror meets creature feature examines the brutality of nature, the hunger of a cryptid, and the immeasurable darkness inside us."

—Rae Knowles, author of *The Stradivarius* and *Merciless Waters*

"*Sawtooth* is everything I want in a horror story. Isolated wilderness setting? Check. Suspenseful, dread-rich writing that kept me locked in from the first line to the last? Check. Characters that completely captured my heart? Check. A monster that lives rent-free in my head? Check. Do not miss this one, but I strongly suggest that you don't bring it camping with you."

—Noelle W. Ihli, author of *Ask for Andrea*

"A harrowing head trip into a dark wilderness where the jaws of death are waiting to snap at your heels. Tread carefully."

—Brian McAuley, author of *Curse of the Reaper*

"Steph Nelson's *Sawtooth* will twist your nerves into knots before breathing hot down the back of your neck and sinking its teeth in. An immersive trap of choice and consequence, *Sawtooth* navigates the complexities of loss and the sacrifices made in the name of love."

—RL Meza, Author of *Our Love Will Devour Us*

"*Sawtooth* is a creature feature, yes, and a damn good one at that, but it's also a poignant exploration of loss. Nelson has crafted a beautifully taut thriller here—one unafraid to explore the notion that it's not always the monster we should fear, but rather ourselves."

—Caleb Stephens, author of *Feeders* and *The Girls in the Cabin*

"*Sawtooth* is a gripping story of devotion and survival against worlds both natural and unnatural. Nelson deftly demonstrates how grief can be just as vicious as the monster that stalks these pages."

—J.A.W. McCarthy, Bram Stoker Award and Shirley Jackson Award nominated author of *Sometimes We're Cruel and Other Stories*

"Show up for the thrilling survival horror but stay for the emotional wreckage—this tale is a harrowing journey through grief that's as exhilarating as it is cathartic. Nelson nailed it."

—Sadie Hartmann, author of *101 Horror Books to Read Before You're Murdered*

"Raw with achingly painted grief, *Sawtooth* is a beautifully-paced isolation wilderness horror that hits on every level. Compelling characters, creeping dread, fantastic pacing and brutal horror—Steph Nelson has crafted a hell of a read."

—Laurel Hightower, author of *Crossroads* and *Below*

CHAPTER 1

Gemma's ashes felt heavy inside the backpack. They weren't, Taryn kept telling herself. Ashes were light, and the box holding them was fairly small. Something Amazon might leave on her doorstep if she ordered a jar of coconut oil, or some new tube socks.

Taryn's fingers clenched padded shoulder straps on either side of her collarbone, slipping a bit as sweat slicked fabric while she hiked. Inside the pack were all the usual items for an overnight in the mountains. Tent, sleeping bag, dehydrated meals. Why did it feel so much heavier this time?

Taryn wiped her forehead with grimy finger pads. She'd hiked almost the full eight miles on what Gemma used to call a *dirty trail* because of the loose, dry dust. Each footfall launched fine flecks like shaking out rugs in an abandoned house. Each step an invitation for earth to cling to Taryn's skin where greedy sweat and tears could soak it up, turning it into a thin layer of mud.

Taryn was almost to her destination: the trailhead for a five-mile out and back hike to the alpine lake. She planned to make camp for the night once she reached the trailhead, then set out in the morning to scatter Gemma's ashes at the lake. Assuming she didn't spend hours there, she should be able to do the day hike in enough time to return to camp by tomorrow evening. Then she'd spend another night, and in the morning, take the eight-mile hike in the dirt back to her car. The plan had been perfect until she saw a brown sign affixed to the main trailhead map.

The sign had a slash through a stick-figure with a backpack and walking stick. *No hiking*. It looked official, and someone had placed a small log across the trail as an added indicator.

Taryn clasped her fingers together on top of her head, trying to get more air into her lungs, and looked up at the sky. "What now?" she said out loud, dropping her arms to her sides, limp. She imagined the look on Gemma's face. Raised eyebrows that communicated, *You're talking to yourself again.*

And then a scene came to mind, from their final backpacking trip together. They were sitting on the side of the trail where Taryn had slipped and cut her knee. Gemma was bandaging it even though Taryn insisted she was fine. It was only a tiny cut and it wasn't like Gemma to fuss over something so small. *Get over it* was more her mode.

"You know why they call these the Sawtooth Mountains, right?" Gemma had said after washing away the blood in order to affix the bandage.

"Because the treeless mountain peaks look like a mouth with sharp teeth," Taryn had said.

"Nope. They're actually named after a monster with teeth shaped like a saw. Sharp as razor blades. Called the Sawtooth."

"Whatever."

Gemma's tendency to tease had been charming when they first met, flirty even. But after seventeen years together, it was annoying as hell.

"The Sawtooth feeds on small rodents, rabbits, mule deer. Unless it catches the scent of something else, something bigger, tastier."

"Stop it, babe. I hate it when you do this."

"I'm not kidding!" Gemma had laughed, applying Neosporin.

"Well, why haven't we seen it then?"

"My uncle saw it when he was a boy."

"Your uncle lives in Colorado."

"He came up to Idaho one summer."

"So, your uncle saw this creature but your mom didn't?" Taryn was trying to prove that Gemma was inventing this story, prodding at it to get her to crack.

"Mom didn't go. She was too young. It was just my uncle and his grandparents."

"I don't even think there were official trails in the Sawtooth Mountains until around the time we were born," Taryn didn't know for sure, but it felt true and maybe it'd crumple Gemma's logic.

"Oh my grandparents didn't need official trails. Trust me. In fact, I'm almost certain they hiked this exact trail." Gemma's words had slowed at the end, to emphasize it, making it creepier.

"Please stop," Taryn said, standing up. "You know that's the only thing I'll be thinking about until we're in the car driving out of here."

"I know, that's the idea." Gemma laughed, nudging Taryn. "Maybe you'll sleep extra close to me tonight."

Taryn stared at the sign now, willing it to not be there. What she wouldn't give to have Gemma around to make some wisecrack about the trail being closed. Get Taryn to laugh about whoever's job it was to go around shutting down trails for seemingly no reason. Tears pinched at her face, but she wiped them with a dusty backhand and focused on what to do next.

Her first instinct was to obey the sign. Turn around, try again next summer. But this had been Gemma's urgent request. To be scattered at this particular alpine lake in the Sawtooth Mountains. One last hike together.

Taryn didn't give a shit about one last hike together. She'd rather have a marble headstone at a green-trimmed cemetery to visit. Just do it the normal way. But Gemma didn't do anything the normal way. *Of course* Gemma would make her go into the mountains as a last wish. And of course the damn trail would be closed, forcing Taryn to choose whether or not to continue, tempting her to turn around and forget about the whole thing. It wasn't like Gemma would know whether her ashes were scattered at the lake or not. But no, Taryn couldn't give in and choose her own way. Not this time.

Taryn looked up at the sky again. Early evening. She'd only mentally prepared to come this far today. Hiking another eight miles back to the car on the fly, in the dark no less, felt like something only Gemma would do. But even if Taryn could channel her inner Gemma and hike back to the car, then what? Would she take Gemma's ashes home? Plop them down on a side table and microwave a burrito for dinner like nothing had happened? Let another year tick by until it was warm enough to come up here again? It had been bad enough that she couldn't force herself to open up the cardboard box. Not even to pour the ashes into a beautiful urn to display on their mantle. She should have done that the first week after Gemma's service. Yet, something had kept her from it until it was impossible to look at that damn box at all. For almost a year, her wife's ashes had sat in the guest room, on the floor, the door closed. A holding pattern until the snow melted enough that she could honor Gemma's outlandish wishes.

She could still camp tonight and then hike back to the car in the morning. But the thought of returning home with Gemma's ashes was a gut punch. She couldn't do it.

The trail ahead seemed fine, at least as far as she could tell leaning over the log to peek. She'd checked online before driving up. But now that she thought about it, there had been nobody on the eight miles up to the trailhead either. Fifteen years ago that would be normal, but not these days. Idaho was crawling with people who craved the outdoors, and they had multiplied exponentially every summer. It was a weekday, so less people due to that, sure. But not a single person? She should have noticed that. Been skeptical. It was like everyone except her knew the hike to the lake was closed. But there were no earlier warnings, and no fires nearby. Not like two summers ago when they'd planned to take this trail, but changed course and camped closer to Stanley after wildfire had ripped through the area.

That October, Gemma's diagnosis ripped through their lives.

It would probably be fine. It was just a day hike. Still, Taryn hesitated. Ignoring the sign's warning felt uncomfortable, like putting on wet jeans.

It's so on brand for you to avoid breaking the rules even when there's nobody here who cares, Gemma said in her mind. Taryn pictured her smile, the way her sun-worn skin dimpled at the corners of her mouth so it looked like tiny parentheses.

She couldn't take Gemma back home. This was where she belonged, where she had wanted to be. And Taryn owed her. God, how she owed her.

You feel so much. I love that about you, Gemma again.

"Too much. I feel too goddamn much," Taryn muttered out loud. She didn't deserve the luxury of sympathy, even from Gemma in her mind.

"Fuck it. We're doing this," Taryn said, stepping over the downed log, then looked over the area for a spot to set up camp.

CHAPTER 2

It was Taryn who had talked Gemma into a more domesticated existence in Boise. Gemma had grown up in Garden Valley, a tiny town at the juncture of the South and Middle Forks of the Payette River in Idaho. It wasn't far from Boise, a little over an hour, but it might as well have been a world away. Garden Valley was a quiet little town filled with natural hot springs, and everything the mountains and river could offer. It had gotten into Gemma, groomed her for a life outdoors.

At first, Taryn thought she too could live in the mountains. Have some cozy cabin in the woods. She didn't need anything but Gemma back then. Back when love was newborn. Had Gemma insisted in those early years, Taryn would have done it. She could imagine summers on the porch with a book. Fresh mountain air. Christmases snowed in. Firelight illuminating frosty windows peering out into pine covered in white. The realization that she could, in fact, never live in the mountains began as a slow creep, starting with, *I need to finish my master's degree.* Then it became, *I have to stay in Boise for this internship.* Looking back now, she had been stalling. She'd never promised Gemma they'd move to the mountains. Not exactly. It was more like she never bothered to correct her when Gemma talked about it. Taryn worried that living in Boise would be a deal breaker for Gemma. Still, she craved success, had to have it. Needed paychecks in dollar amounts she only imagined while growing up.

When Taryn landed a job with a dream agency, she knew for sure she wouldn't leave town. The salary was irresistible, and she couldn't work a PR job in the mountains where there was no service, after all. That's when fresh mountain air transformed into the bother of driving a hundred miles just to shop at Costco. Idyllic

Christmas in a cabin became the horror of being snowed in for months with only a snowmobile to get in and out. She had never shared this with Gemma, only smiled and nodded when her wife talked over the years about *someday*.

When Taryn broke the news that she'd accepted the position at the agency, Gemma didn't react, wouldn't really talk about it. Just said that they would make it work.

"I only need to stay until my career is set," Taryn promised. "Maybe I can get on as a contractor with an even bigger firm, based out of L.A., or New York City or something. If we can get internet out where you want to be, I could work from home. You never know."

"You never know," Gemma had repeated. But what did that mean? Gemma had always been a little hard to read. Taryn couldn't tell if she was mad, or not. If she was joking, or not. She came to assume that Gemma was *not* mad in general, and that she *was* joking in general. But on this one thing, this issue of living in Boise for possibly forever, Taryn simply didn't believe Gemma could *not* be mad. And what if she was? Would she leave? Gemma was the glue that held Taryn together. She couldn't—wouldn't—imagine a life without her.

But Taryn couldn't live in the mountains either, so she was stuck in this charade with Gemma, pretending that they'd eventually move into the wilderness.

Gemma took a part-time job at REI. She said it was for the benefits and friendships. But they didn't need the money, so why bother? Gemma was capable of so much more. Why didn't she want to do something with her forestry degree? Taryn had even told Gemma that if she wanted to take a ranger position or, at the minimum, a camp host job during the summer, that was fine. Taryn would come visit every weekend if need be. But Gemma just shrugged and said she liked her job. Wanted to keep her schedule flexible because Taryn's was so demanding. *I like being together*, Gemma had said.

Taryn was secretly so relieved at this. Their unspoken agreement—*being together is the most important thing*—sustained them. Even if it was Gemma giving and Taryn taking a lot of the time. But as long as Gemma was happy, what was the harm? Plus, Gemma still spent days off, weeks at a time in the mountains. While most partners were fussy about the other one going away for long stretches, Taryn was glad. Of course she missed Gemma, but she was thrilled to see her wife get an escape from *Taryn's life*. This was how Taryn began referring to it in her mind. Never letting on to Gemma, for fear that Gemma would call her to account and require Taryn to *do* something about it. Fix it. Make it *their life*.

This only made it worse, and soon Taryn imagined Gemma secretly angry with her, but non-confrontational enough to keep it to herself. Fear cut into Taryn's heart, festered there over the years, despite that she tried to shake it free every time it snaked cold tentacles around her mind. One time Gemma complained about living in Boise. "I feel stuck here, like an insect in a glass jar. I need to be free."

This triggered Taryn. "But I'm the one who pays the bills. You want me to just not work?"

"I don't need all this shit," Gemma shouted, arms waving around. "This is all you. It doesn't even feel like a home to me, except that you're here."

There it was: Gemma's resentment. Taryn had known it was there all along. The worst part was Gemma was right. They didn't *need* all of this. But Taryn wanted it all. And more. She had grown up poor, hiding in the bathroom during lunch in elementary school so nobody would see that she didn't have anything to eat. Until one teacher figured it out and helped her get on the free lunch program. Mom would take her shopping at Kmart, let her put new clothes, shoes, in the shopping cart, make her think this time she'd buy it all for Taryn. But Mom would start crying in the checkout lane and Taryn knew. She couldn't afford any of it and they'd leave the store, Taryn looking over her shoulder at the abandoned cart full of new things, growing smaller and smaller. They'd end up at Goodwill weeks after school began instead, her mom painstakingly pushing coins across the checkout counter to pay. Taryn praying in her heart that there were enough coins. This, only after her mom was fed up with Taryn coming home in tears over what other kids said about her too-short jeans. Her graying Keds knock-offs, soles flopping, a rubber mouth announcing with every step that Taryn was poor. Dirty, white trash.

"Go live in the mountains then," came out of Taryn's mouth before she could think. Immediately, she regretted it. Wanted to erase the words before they reached Gemma, but anger wouldn't allow it. Her heart shrieked inside, demanded that she take it back, but her body, her mouth, wouldn't budge.

Gemma's jaw had dropped. "Are you serious? Why would you say that? I'd never leave you."

Taryn's relief at that had been overwhelming and she vowed never to suggest it again. If Gemma wasn't willing to go, was it really Taryn's job to force her? She must not be that upset with *Taryn's life.*

But the gnawing feeling grew. This sense that she had more, gotten her way more frequently than Gemma. She had love plus her career. Gemma just had love. And why couldn't Taryn just give in? Because she needed to take violent swipes at her deep well of need? Prove to eight-year-old her that they were fine now? That money somehow made them safe? Even realizing these dynamics, Taryn couldn't make a move to rectify them. It didn't matter anyway, Gemma never brought it up again. She was content.

Or so it seemed. Yet Gemma constantly fidgeted with her wedding ring, spinning, spinning, spinning it, while zoning out. Something about that gold ring—it had been Gemma's mother's. In their family for years. She insisted on wearing it instead of the massive diamond Taryn wanted to buy for her. Taryn imagined the ring absorbing all of Gemma's angst about their life, like Gemma drew comfort from it, placing all her anger into it while it spun. In return, Gemma received the ability to go on. To happily live *Taryn's life*. An exchange. But at what cost?

Taryn was prone to reading into things, but still, it was like she could feel the friction of the ring against Gemma's fingers. The warmth against skin, growing into something dark, something that could consume her. Screaming into a void, *This isn't what I signed up for. You tricked me. You have what you want, and I don't. I'm only here because I can't leave you. I love you too much.*

Love was never the problem between them.

When Taryn reminded Gemma she was doing it again, Gemma always apologized. *Just fidgeting, sorry.* Taryn couldn't bring herself to ask what Gemma thought about while she worked that ring. She was afraid of the answer.

CHAPTER 3

When the sun broke through darkness and turned the hood of stars over the Sawtooth Mountains invisible, Taryn was already awake. Already dressed, sitting beside the small fire pan that cradled a warm flame. Summer in the Sawtooths was cold enough to need socks at night, but hot enough to peel down to a sports bra during the day. She sipped her second cup of instant coffee and watched the steam rise from her tiny mug. A last indulgence before setting out.

Taryn wouldn't need all her gear today, and since her mind was already on the task at hand, she shook the dregs out of the collapsible mug in one quick motion and brushed dirt off her rear.

Inside the tent, Taryn detached the lid of her backpack. It converted into a small day pack that looked like a bookbag for a preschooler. She'd return to camp in time to crash for the night and then hike back to the car in the morning, so she wouldn't need much. Water, filter, and a protein bar would do. Taryn had already eaten an entire Mountain House meal and that would hold her over for hours. Total gut bomb. Was she missing anything? The ashes, of course. Shit, this trip really was off to a great start. First the closed trail, now she almost forgot to bring along the entire reason for being up there. She added the small box to her pack, but the cardboard was awkward and made it so she couldn't zip the thing shut.

Should have worked that out back at home, dumbass.

Taryn took the plastic bag of ashes out of the box. The top was tied, so she set it into the pack. It fit. The pack was bulky, full. Not ideal for hiking, but then again, it was just a quick out and back. She'd done enough of these day hikes that she wasn't too concerned.

Slow down. What else am I missing?

A maxi pad. She'd brought a few in the big pack just in case. Knowing her luck, especially on this trip, she'd start her period out in the middle of nowhere. Her cycle had a mind of its own and she'd given up trying to anticipate its arrival decades ago. She brought supplies everywhere she went, and now she was just hanging on for menopause. A maxi pad weighed almost nothing, and doing without it would be far worse than carrying it along and finding that she didn't need it after all. She stuffed one yellow square into the pack.

Next, she held her phone. It only had one bar of service. No way it'd get service much further out. She could bring it with her, but why bother? Gemma never brought her phone hiking. Always left it in the car. Taryn wasn't as experienced of a hiker as Gemma, but she could find her way around a five mile out and back without needing to call the cavalry. Just then, the phone's one bar disappeared like it was trying to have a say in the matter. Now there was no reason to bring it.

Taryn dropped the phone. Hard plastic landed on the tent's floor, muffled by her sleeping bag. Gemma's voice was in her mind. *Atta girl. Live for the moment.*

"You're a bad influence," she said out loud to Gemma, but a bloom of pride grew inside as she imagined how proud Gemma would be to see her leaving the phone behind. She reached down for her empty mug, tossed it into the tent and pulled the zipper shut. It was time to get started. Even if she wasn't ready. She'd never be ready to say goodbye, but she was there, doing this for Gemma anyway.

There really couldn't be a better day to be outside, either. The expanse of sky was clear, not a cloud. She put on the small backpack and set out. The trail followed a river about twenty feet wide. Water carved a valley through the mountains. Suddenly, the 3,000-foot elevation gain made sense. Yesterday's hike had been mostly flat, just an inroad to this. Today, Taryn would be hiking what looked like a thin shelf that cut into the side of the mountain, about a hundred feet above the river. This side was shady with growth. Pine trees, tall grass, and purple lupine carpeted the incline on her right. There were boulders with white intrusions visible even from a distance. Crows on a low branch watched her. Cawed at something. She couldn't see what it was. Golden butterflies danced circles around each other like a single unit. They passed in front of her in a flyby before bounding over the edge and down toward the river. It was early, so the air was refreshing, but without that edge of cool. It would be a hot day.

At least this trail was nothing like the dusty hike the day before. She hadn't washed off yesterday's grime, but her Smartwool long johns and sleeping bag had wiped most of it away during the night. What was left felt chalky and dry to the touch. Maybe she'd take a dip in the lake when she got there. Gemma would approve.

Taryn surveyed the other side of the river where the trail back to camp was located. She'd take that trail when she was ready to leave the lake. The other side looked really desolate though, with a bit of brush where the mountain met river, but otherwise rocky all the way to the peak. There was a solitary boulder or tree here and there, but otherwise, it was bare. No matter. Not like she'd be sightseeing on the return trip. She'd probably just be crying the whole time anyway. Might as well take the ugly way home. Back to her empty house, to live her ugly life without Gemma.

Plus, Gemma would want her to take the other trail home. She wouldn't stick to the pretty side. She'd challenge herself, make discoveries along the way. So, that's what Taryn would do this time too, in Gemma's honor.

Taryn made good time, only stopping to drink water, and judging by the sun's placement, it was before noon when she reached the small alpine lake. Jagged peaks on all sides cradled the water, bits of winter's snow still lodged in the highest crevices despite the heat. These mountain lakes always reminded her of a massive jewel embedded in rock. Something between an emerald and a blue topaz.

"The color of your eyes," Gemma had said once. Taryn had fake gagged, which made Gemma laugh. She never could tell if Gemma was serious or not.

A few pine trees speckled the base of the mountains, almost touching the waterline in places, but not many. Most trees were stripped of branches, needles, and their trunks looked like enormous gray and black toothpicks aimed at the sky, courtesy of a past wildfire.

Taryn dropped her bag next to a flat rock and sat down. She took big swigs of water, no longer trying to conserve it. She ate the protein bar. Peanut butter chocolate, Gemma's favorite. Taryn hated that flavor, but Gemma had practically cleaned Costco out of them just before her diagnosis. Now the nasty things were creeping up on their expiration date and Taryn couldn't let them go to waste. There were some things about growing up poor that were impossible to shake, no matter how much you tried.

Taryn took another drink, and when the water bottle was almost empty, she walked along the rocky shore of the lake until she found a good spot to fill it up again. She dipped it in like a ladle and scooped up an entire bottle full. The pressure to take care of Gemma's ashes pushed on her from the inside, an urge. The lake looked inviting, and it was quite hot out. She thought about swimming again. But maybe it'd be better to get on with it. Get back to camp.

Why? So I can hurry up and be alone again?

The expanse of lake was a perfect glassy mirror reflecting mountains and white clouds, brush stroked onto the sky. The sun zeroed in on her, as if concentrating its heat. A little chipmunk ran along the shore a distance away, its tiny pads scrambling across the smallest stones. Birds sang. Taryn's eyes explored the bottom of the lake. It was shallow and she could see through the glass. Rocks and waterlogged branches were submerged in a kaleidoscope on the lake floor, inviting her gaze further out. Her eyes came to rest on something that stood in stark contrast with the rest of the debris. Something that didn't fit in.

Taryn was on a rock, leaning forward to get a better view. It looked like one of the branches, yes, but it wasn't dark. Instead, it gleamed white against the sunlight. Straining to see was no good, and she couldn't tell what it was, or if it was even worth all this effort. Just because the other branches in the water were dark didn't mean they all were. Maybe it was a different kind of wood. Not pine. Aspen or something.

She hopped down off the rock and set her water bottle on the shore. God, it was hot. Maybe a skinny dip was worth the hassle. The water was so pristine, how could she pass up the chance?

That and I doubt you'll ever see another alpine lake in your life, Gemma said in her mind.

It was true. Taryn had no desire to backpack after this. She didn't even feel sad about it. First though, she wanted to take care of Gemma's ashes. Nothing else mattered right then.

CHAPTER 4

Taryn felt calm, almost numb, as she worked open the bag's plastic knot. She was surprised when tears didn't come. It wasn't like the pain of loss was gone. But maybe the waves of grief had pounded those boulders into fine sand, and all that was left was for her to stand there, dig her toes into it. Maybe after so many months of daily sobbing, this was the point when things would even out. When she would no longer be pummeled by a sneaker wave of sorrow at the most random, inconvenient times.

With the bag open, Taryn stared down into the ash, and something burst to life inside her. Something new, different. A powerful longing so foreign that she produced an inappropriate little laugh when she should have been overcome with sadness.

She wanted to touch the ashes. Touch *her*. One last time. Then the tears came, and Taryn chastised herself for thinking she was through with the crying. Still, she had to take some of Gemma's ashes in her hand. There was nothing else to do right then. She wanted to hold her wife again, feel for any essence of Gemma that might still be in those remnants of bone.

Taryn placed her fingers inside the bag. Moved them around slowly, so as not to create a big poof. She found the bottom. And something else. Something hard.

It was smooth, a circle.

Taryn knew what it was before she saw it, but in a breath she had it out and on display in front of her eyes.

Gemma's wedding ring.

What the hell?

She held it up next to her own ringed finger. An incongruent pair that fit together anyway.

But how had it gotten into Gemma's ashes? Surely the funeral home hadn't forgotten to remove it before cremating her body. And if they had, wouldn't it have melted? If not, surely, they would have noticed while processing the ashes, or pouring them into the bag. Talk about an oversight. That was three levels worth of fuck ups on the funeral home's part. And after Taryn had asked specifically about the ring during Gemma's open casket service. Then once more when she picked up the ashes.

They had said they didn't have it. Hadn't seen it. Taryn would have used her boss lady voice to press them, make them find it. But that day she was too tired. Beyond spent. She told them she'd reach out in a few weeks. Instead, she asked Gemma's dad to follow up. After many unsuccessful attempts, they'd concluded that the ring was simply gone. He was just as heartbroken as Taryn had been, as the ring was his wife's and meant a lot to their family. Had been worn by their women for generations.

Taryn wiped ashy fingers across her eyes, trying to see through tears. "And you were with me the whole time," she whispered to the ring.

Taryn blew at it to remove the dust, and slipped it on to her right hand. Gemma was so much smaller than her, so the ring only fit her pinky.

Now to the matter of scattering the ashes. It felt doable, like Taryn's dread had disappeared with the discovery of the ring.

But Taryn suddenly realized that if she dumped the contents of the bag out, they'd make a pile on the ground. That felt weird. It wasn't how she imagined it would be. Or how it was in the movies where the wind picked up the loved one's remains, dispersing them perfectly into nature while some ballad played loud in the background.

Hell, Tare, just toss them. Big Lebowski style. Who cares if you look like The Dude when it's all done? Gemma said in her mind.

Taryn cry-laughed. It had been Gemma's favorite movie.

Still, she couldn't do it. Instead, she found a stick and dug a hole next to a tree. Away from the shore so nobody would accidentally step on it. She saved out a small handful of ashes, just to have the experience of tossing them, even if the only thing in her mind now was Jeff Bridges, covered in ashes.

And then, like the universe had read her thoughts, the sun winked when a puffy cloud moved over it. A breeze pushed up against her back and she held out her fist, opened it. The ashes floated out toward the lake.

"Goodbye, Gem."

Not goodbye, goodnight. Gemma was in her mind. *I'll sleep when I'm dead.*

It would be so Gemma to crack one joke after another. Especially in these serious moments.

"Selfish humor, Gem. Nobody thinks that's funny except you." Taryn whispered her standard reply to Gemma's inappropriate joking. But God, what she wouldn't give to have Gemma there, pushing her buttons to the point of irritation again.

Taryn couldn't wait to get into the water now. A burden was lifted, a momentary reprieve from grief. She took off boots, peeled merino wool socks off both feet. Then she shucked her thin tank top, breathable shorts, bra, underwear. Her first steps in broke the lake's perfect sheen, sending ripples out like fish jumping. She stood until the movement stopped and icy water gripped her ankles.

Then Taryn got all the way in, didn't bother with wading. It was too cold for that. You had to take the freezing punishment all at once. The body adjusts. Gemma taught her that. She let out a big gasp when she came up. Cold was an understatement.

Taryn treaded water then dunked her head under again, smoothed her hair back from her forehead as she whipped her legs to stay afloat.

It was surreal to still be able to see the bottom of the lake even when she couldn't touch it. She'd stirred up the silty floor a bit when she walked in, but it was settling now, and once again she looked below.

That white branch was directly underneath her. And next to it, another object the same shade of white, but rounded. Actually, there were quite a few of those white branches down there. She thought about diving to retrieve one, find out what it was, but just then, something broke the quiet on the opposite side of the lake.

A spill of rocks down the mountain. She saw the last bits making way for the shore, but couldn't tell what had caused the slide.

Her stomach jumped in panic. She wasn't alone.

She watched intently for long enough to satisfy her fear. She saw nothing and after all, if it was something to worry about, it couldn't have run away that fast. A large animal would take longer to disappear than something small, something harmless. She'd looked up right when she heard the rocks, and hadn't seen anything.

Probably just another chipmunk.

Taryn returned her attention to the lake bottom. It wouldn't exactly be wise to dive down and inspect; she should probably save her energy for the trek home. But something about the way those objects caught the sun...

Her skin was numb, fingers so cold it was hard to make a fist. She had to get out soon.

But Gemma would want to know what those white sticks were.

Her first dive was unsuccessful and she had to tread longer to wait for the silt floor to settle.

The second time, she stayed under long enough not to miss. Her fingers wrapped around one of the longer objects, and she tucked her body to plant feet on the bottom. Her toes squidged silty mud, but her eyes were up, focused on blazing rays of sun inside wrinkles of water that called her toward oxygen. Her feet fluttered hard and just when she thought her lungs would burst, her head broke the boundary of wet underneath and she came up, sucking for air.

Taryn shook her head so she could see through wet eyes. The stick was very white. Long, but not as long as the dark branches had been. It had two knobby ends.

This wasn't a stick at all. It was a bone.

"Shit!" Taryn threw the bone back into the water. It looked human. Like a femur.

She scrambled to get out, and Gemma's voice was in her mind.

It's probably just an animal bone. Deer, sheep, even cows have bones that can look human. Why do you always go to the worst possible scenario?

"Yes, true. It's probably not human," Taryn whispered, forcing herself to agree with Gemma in her mind while dripping across the shore toward her clothes.

Unless that was why the trail was closed. Because some hiker went missing. Some stupid backpacker. Someone like her who would ignore the sign, choosing this one time in their whole life to be a rule breaker.

But no. People go missing in the wilderness all the time. Plus, even if it were a missing hiker, they've been dead long enough to decompose completely. Water this cold would act like a freezer, take so much longer for anything to deteriorate.

The water.

Taryn's stomach clenched as she looked at her water bottle full of lake, standing there on the shore. She picked it up, peered through blue-tinted plastic, like trying to see invisible rotting corpse microbes. No reason to worry, since she had a filter. Although, gross, still. She set the bottle down and pulled on her underwear, fumbled with her sports bra, getting it caught momentarily on her wet back.

Once she was dressed, Taryn pulled the filter out of her bag. A spendy little gadget that Gemma had splurged on. It was shaped like a pen and filtered the water by UV light. She stuck it into the water bottle and pushed the blue button. Nothing happened. She pushed it again. Nothing.

Taryn pulled the filter out of the water and looked it over, shook it. It worked just this morning. She opened the handle, like she was going to change the batteries, but that was stupid. If the batteries were dead, she didn't have any extra. Did Gemma bring extra when they backpacked? Did Gemma bring a backup filter? She'd never noticed. Gemma always took care of everything when they went out together.

Taryn pulled all four double-A batteries out, arranged them differently, like it was some magic trick. When she pushed the button again, the filter turned on. Then immediately went off.

Fuck. She sat down. No water. Not a drop until she got back to camp.

It's not the end of the world. You'll be thirsty, but you can make it back without water, Gemma said.

Was that Gemma's actual survival advice, or was it just Taryn's wishful thinking? She knew for a fact she could not drink this water. Diarrhea would only turn the threat of dehydration from a possibility into a true inevitability.

She shoved the filter back into her bag. She'd try it again later. It only needed to run for sixty seconds to work. Maybe she could squeeze a minute out of the batteries. *Could it be a cumulative minute or did it have to be one long minute, seconds ticking side-by-side?* God, why didn't she bring—

An animal howled, interrupting her thoughts.

Taryn startled, looked around, and then walked along the shore until she reached the trail. She knew that howl. How could she have forgotten about the wolves out there?

CHAPTER 5

The U.S. government reintroduced wolves into the Sawtooth Mountains in 1995, and had been sending biologists to study the pack ever since. In fact, several summers ago, Taryn and Gemma had camped right next to a whole crew of government biologists who had set up a base and were taking trips deep into the mountains to study them.

Gemma had gone over to their campfire that time with a six-pack and an ulterior motive to find out more about where the dens were. She wanted to see wolf pups in the wild, even if from a distance. But after a couple beers, the biologists were still politely demurring at all of her pointed questions.

"Gem, I don't think they can tell us where the wolf dens are," Taryn had whispered eventually, wondering if Gemma realized she'd asked the same question over and over. That she was awkwardly repeating herself. It wasn't like her, and she hadn't even had a single beer.

"It's true," a female biologist said when she overheard Taryn's comment. "I'm so sorry, we aren't supposed to share any of that information. Not that you would go and disturb their environment, but you know some people would."

Gemma had nodded in agreement. It made sense, but Taryn could tell by the shimmer in her wife's brown eyes, she still wanted to find it.

She'd brought it up the next day. "Let's look for a wolf den."

The prospect had terrified Taryn, but Gemma reassured her, "It'd just be the babies. The adults are all out hunting food, remember what the biologists said?"

But the biologists hadn't said that. They said some were out hunting but some stayed behind to watch over the pups. How could Gemma have remembered it so wrong? That had bothered Taryn because she could tell Gemma genuinely didn't recall it correctly. These were some of the first signs of Gemma's disease even though neither of them knew it. At the time, all Taryn could think was the last thing she wanted to run into was a couple of wolves, slightly hungry, and trying to protect their babies.

And just like that, wolves were circling deep inside Taryn's mind.

Shit.

Taryn had gone about a quarter of the way on the return trail thinking about the wolves and bones in the lake. She hadn't heard any howling, but still, that didn't mean she was safe. She'd also spent hours thinking about how thirsty she was. Wondering what the signs of dehydration were. Thirst, yes, but what next? She was still sweating, so that had to be a good sign. Or not. If she was sweating, it meant she was losing water. But at least she still *could* sweat. Right?

Why the hell hadn't she taken the shadier side back? She'd gotten it into her mind that she would take the trail back the way it was designed, the way Gemma would do it. But she should have re-evaluated that once she discovered there was zero water to drink. And then, if she wasn't stressed enough over all of this, her mind brought back that stupid creature Gemma had teased her about. The Sawtooth. She tried to pivot her brain, but there was too much to avoid thinking about. Every attempt to change her thoughts away from a distressing issue planted her neck-deep into another one. They circled around her head like cartoon stars after a fall. The wolves, the heat, dehydration, the bones, the fact that this side felt creepier in general than the other side had. She swore it did. And then, being out there alone made the impossible feel real. What if there was such a thing as the Sawtooth?

Stop thinking about it. There's no Sawtooth.

She tried again to replace the intrusive thoughts with something more positive, but her mind failed to rev up and go. There was so little positivity to draw from over the past two years. She was walking faster now, almost running, but she couldn't run or she'd get even thirstier. Could she outrun the thirst? Get back to camp sooner? No, she'd sweat more, lose water faster.

Try the filter again, Gemma said.

Taryn obeyed, stopping abruptly and set it up. She pushed the button. Nothing.

She wanted to scream, to throw the damn thing into the river. Why didn't she bring a hand pump instead? They had all kinds of filters at home. Or a life straw! Just as a backup. For fuck's sake, even a *tampon* would be better than nothing. God knew she had those hanging around all over her house, car. And she'd read in one of those clickbait articles on the web that you could drink water through a tampon applicator in an emergency situation. That the cotton tampon would filter out a lot of the contaminants. But no, she'd brought a maxi pad this time, of course. She swallowed tears as she put everything away, swung the small bag onto her shoulders and kept going.

With every step that touched the downhill slope of the trail, Taryn felt surer that this side of the river was scarier than the other side had been. Even though that was stupid and she had no proof. But it felt like she was being watched. As if the two trails were an angel and a devil on the river's shoulders. For as much green, lush beauty there had been on the way up to the lake, this way offered only rock. Dry, jagged, fist-sized stones. It was scree up to the top, as far as the eye could discern. That, coupled with the heat of early afternoon, gave off a suffocating, stranded feeling. What if a landslide happened right now? She'd get pummeled. Stoned to death like an Old Testament sinner.

But how could this side be that much different? She could see the other side clearly. And yet, she hadn't felt any bad vibes over there. It was probably that this side was uglier and hotter since the day had gotten on. She was more desperate now. Scared.

She kept whipping her head back, expecting to see wolves coming right for her, faster than she could run. *Were they hiding? Waiting for their chance to pounce?* It wasn't possible for anything to hide in broad daylight on her side of the river. There was nothing to hide behind either.

She was visible. Exposed. Not only to the hot sun, but to whatever else was out there. The air was so thick with dread that she could almost feel it in her mouth. The suffocating feeling it gave her when she drew in a breath, like swimming through mud.

What if she turned around and took the other trail? The lake, and the option to walk on the other side of the river was miles in the rearview. Taryn could rehash this path to the lake in order to get on the better trail. Where it hadn't felt creepy, where bushes and trees could give her hiding spots. But no, it was probably two miles back to the lake. By the time she got there, set foot on the pretty trail, she would have done four out of five miles on the creepy side, with another five to do on the safe side. More time out there without water.

But there was no water at camp either! Not without the filter. Taryn let out a little cry of defeat. Her mind whirred trying to plan out what she was going to do for water once she reached camp.

No, don't think about that right now. Focus on getting to camp first. One problem at a time. Plus, I have the phone. One bar is all I need to call for help if things get dire.

Being on the exposed side of the river seemed like a small problem in light of no water, but it was the thing in her face right then. She couldn't stop thinking of ways she might escape the awful trail. Maybe she could cross the river? She looked into it, studying it for a spot to cross. Water rushed fast, pouring over boulders like liquid glass and then exploding into whitecaps. No. It would be too risky to get across. Better to stay over here and push through the last three miles. Whatever had howled—wolves, some crazy person, the Sawtooth—she had to just keep moving.

Nobody's out here. You're overthinking it. Gemma again.

"Nobody unless you count the human remains," Taryn said, and then shivered, despite the heat.

Tare, calm down. You don't even know if that was a person. And then, if it was, couldn't it be a lost hiker? Why does it have to mean you're facing a threat? Gemma said.

"It was a lot of bones. Maybe more than one body. You think a bunch of hikers are getting lost on this day hike?" Taryn said, but wished she hadn't because the last thing she needed was to argue the side of being scared shitless against her dead, and currently very reasonable, wife.

What if she was losing her shit? If she kept on like this, any sense of reason would evaporate in the heat of the day. If she allowed it to continue, put on her seatbelt and went along for the ride, surely *crazy* was the destination. She should listen to the Gemma in her mind.

But what would she do if a wolf came at her? What about a whole pack of them? How would she get away? God, it was so hard to listen to reason right then.

Wolves are more scared of you than you are of them, Gemma said.

"I doubt that," Taryn muttered. She wanted to be grateful for those threads of reason, cling to them like a lifeline, but she didn't believe any of it. It was so like Gemma to downplay her fears right after stoking them with stories about monsters.

Then another cry sounded across the mountains, but this time, it wasn't a wolf.

CHAPTER 6

The cry was more like a bunch of singular voices screaming out as one. Human voices, Taryn swore.

Adrenaline flushed through Taryn's body, took her breath away, knocking her wind out. She was immobile, standing on the trail like a doofus. Chills ran up her body and her mind raced, trying to make sense of that sound. But it couldn't. There was nothing even remotely familiar about that noise. At least not in terms of animals that could be out there.

What the fuck?

She picked up her pace so that she was taking long strides down the sloped trail. When she realized she still had about half the way to go, she ran. Didn't care if she got thirstier. With each step, pressure mounted to go faster. Get away from anything living out there that might threaten her. Wolves, yes, but also, whatever had made that other noise. She didn't want to freak herself out, but she couldn't help it. If it wasn't a wolf, what was it? She kept turning around, now half expecting a wolf—or worse—to be on the trail, in a dead heat toward her.

What did the Sawtooth sound like? No, that was stupid. The Sawtooth wasn't real.

She stopped abruptly when she arrived at a pile of downed logs. How in the world did it get there? The whole trail had been bare and then this. The logs were covering the trail like jackstraws, but she could see where the dirt ribbon path picked up again and wound down further toward safety. Closer to the river. Taryn had to cross over the logs to access the trail again, but she hesitated. She couldn't see what was underneath. It seemed like maybe the trail dipped there, and the logs created an overpass of sorts. Was there a drop off that she'd have to hop down from in order to rejoin the trail? How stable were these logs? Many were blanched white like driftwood and looked rickety.

White like the bones in the lake had been.

But these weren't bones, they were just remains of trees and only one or two looked freshly fallen, sturdy.

She could get on her rear and crabwalk down the rock to the river, but then again, she'd have to cross, and the water was even rougher here. Eddies swirled behind rocks, downed branches hung across from the bank. None that were strong enough to cross over, but instead, placed just right to trap you underneath for a quick drowning. She had to get over these logs on the trail. Why was she hesitating? It felt like the anticipation before cliff jumping, the yes, no, yes, no, yes process. The sort of thing you're not sure you'll actually do until you're doing it. She willed her foot to step up on the first one, but it wouldn't.

Something moved on the other side of the river, out of the corner of her vision.

She scanned the far bank to lock eyes on whatever it was. If she could just see it, she'd feel better. Even if it *was* a wolf, or worse.

What if it was the Sawtooth creature?

"No, that's ridiculous," Taryn whispered. It was probably just another rebellious hiker like her.

It felt good to say those words to herself. To be her own voice of reason. But it only took a few seconds of peering over to the other side to nuke the hope of it being a person. Green brush and wildflowers across the river stretched tall, consuming the sun's light, but nothing else moved. No noise. Nothing human. Definitely not anything that could scream in so many voices at once.

"Stop it," Taryn said out loud. She couldn't let her imagination take charge. She'd already allowed it more freedom than was healthy. She had to keep it together. Put one foot in front of the other and make it back to camp.

The afternoon sun was hot and Taryn's mouth smacked dry. She wiped a hand along the back of her neck. Still sweaty. That good and bad sign that she wasn't dehydrated yet. How long did it take for diarrhea to set in after drinking contaminated water? She only needed another hour, maybe two and she'd be back at camp. She could handle a bout of diarrhea once she had the phone and had made a call for help. Her gut was still telling her not to drink the water, but it was torture.

Stressing about dehydration gave her a moment's reprieve from thinking about wolves, or the Sawtooth. But once she made the decision not to drink, she was right back to those thoughts. Her eyes watched the other side of the river for movement again. Had she imagined it?

Make noise, Gemma said. *Being loud is safer than trying to sneak around. You might scare predators away.*

"Worth a try," she shouted, but once the words were born, they felt alien. They didn't belong there at all, and the roaring river gulped up the volume anyway. She was left trying to think up something else to yell. Another way to make noise. Nothing came to mind. Not only that, but something deep inside said not to be loud right then. She didn't want to draw attention. Disturb *things*.

She lifted a foot and balanced it on the first piece of timber. It was about the width of her shoe and it seemed steady, so she reached for a stick poking up, wedged in upright. Her hand touched smooth, barkless wood and she tugged a bit. It held, so she pulled herself up. Looking down, darkness reigned in the tight crevices between logs. She couldn't see how far the distance was between the logs and the trail. It didn't seem wide enough to fall through, but it was sure wide enough for something to reach up and grab her ankle.

Nothing's going to reach up, Gemma said.

Taryn nodded in agreement and took another step across.

A bush on the other side of the river shook hard, pulled her attention away.

"Who's there?" Taryn shouted, holding her arms out for balance. Her heart careened into her throat, thumping blood into her ears. Eyes craving to uncover the threat. Just to see it. Make it better. Taryn wobbled with the effort it took to quickly but thoroughly scan the other side. She had to push her balance forward, use the shifty momentum to step on the next log, or she'd fall off. Or worse, fall through. Then she saw that some of the gaps were certainly large enough for body parts to fit. Not that she'd fall to her death below. It was only a few inches, a foot at most above the trail, but plenty of space for a leg to slip in and crack in half.

Slow steps. Focus on something ahead and don't look down, Gemma said.

Maybe she should make some noise again. Make her presence larger.

Taryn began to hum a tune, and when that felt comfortable, she bellowed out the lyrics to "Brown-Eyed Girl" by Van Morrison. Gemma was the one with the brown eyes, but she'd always said it was her song for Taryn.

The next log was thinner. Since she was shaking, trying to yell words to a song, she landed a foot with more force than she meant. Still, it held.

Another step and her legs were spread for balance. One of the wider gaps of black darkness was squarely between her feet.

"Nothing's going to reach up." She repeated Gemma's encouragement in a whisper and then went back to singing.

An ear-splitting crack rang out on the other side of the river. Branches—no, larger than that. Boughs breaking.

Taryn's mouth clamped shut, silenced the song. She tore her gaze away from the focal point ahead, searching the other bank to find the source of noise. Again, she couldn't see anything capable of making it.

Bright lasers of sunlight through pine trees highlighted wildflowers and tall grass. She put an arm up, bent her elbow so her forearm could shade her eyes.

Nothing, nothing, nothing and then…

A shadow flashed from behind a robust pine.

CHAPTER 7

Before Taryn could figure out what the hell it was, the shadow ducked behind the tree. No way it was human, that was for damn sure. It was too tall. The way it moved was unnatural, almost jerky. Reminded her of those haunted houses during Halloween where someone walked around in a dark room with a strobe light on to scare people.

Then shadowy hands emerged, braced against the tree. More than two.

The log underneath Taryn's feet wavered, slipped a bit as if readjusting its position to hold her weight. Her balance went wonky, and even though she hadn't looked at the other side long enough to feel satisfied, she fixed her eyes straight ahead in order to regain her footing. As her body stopped wavering, she saw those jerky movements in her peripheral again.

She didn't look over right away. Had to keep her eyes on the focal point to make sure her feet were squarely planted first. But once they were, she whipped her head to see, still straddling two logs.

Nothing.

She was only a third of the way across the pile, and she should tread carefully, but her need to be on solid ground, to get back to camp, vetoed caution. Taryn ran across the logs. Too fast. Her momentum got away from her. Her body was pushing to go, get the hell away, but her feet hesitated about *where* to go. Where to land. This disconnect broke the timing of her steps. At the last log, she didn't reach far enough with her foot. Taryn stepped when she should have leapt, and just before touchdown, everything slowed and her brain registered that she was going to miss. Her foot was heading right for the gap between logs. The ball of her foot snagged on the smallest branch jutting sideways out of that final log. Then her whole leg was swallowed by black space. Her foot hit hard pack below. She heard a pop.

Taryn screamed.

She tried to catch her breath, but it felt like drowning. She couldn't get air into her lungs fast enough. Shock thoughts told her this wasn't her voice screaming. Didn't sound anything like her. But the searing pain in her leg, the audible pop of her own bone, said otherwise.

Finally, oxygen caught up with her gasping. There she was, one leg crammed between logs up to her knee. The other one was bent, kneeling on the last log, like in prayer. This one dug into bark as it did all the work supporting her weight. Her hands throbbed hot against the wood's rough skin as she braced herself. They were scraped, but not bleeding. The only thing Taryn could think about was how easy it would have been to topple forward as her foot went between those logs. Snap her shin in half. But that hadn't happened. She would know if that had happened, right?

She couldn't see the hidden leg, so she tried to wiggle it to confirm it wasn't broken. That was a mistake.

She screamed again. Taryn had to pull her leg out, but how? She couldn't tell for sure where the source of pain was. It all hurt. There was probably a pretty big injury down there in the darkness, but the thing that hurt the most right then were the scrapes along her leg. The bark had raked skin on the way down. They were probably the least of her worries.

She leaned forward on her knee, still bracing against the log with her hands. When she thought she had her balance, she pulled the bad leg out. Too fast. She screamed again.

The meatiest part of her calf had gotten caught on some branch hidden under the logs. It keyed a gash the whole length, only relenting at the high top of her hiking boot. Looking behind, trying to assess the damage, she saw her own flesh folded slightly outward at the cut. Like tugging a zipper open. Her foot was stuck now, and the pressure of wood against it was excruciating.

Still, she had to get that foot unwedged.

Taryn turned the foot sideways to line it up with the gap in the logs. That was when she knew for certain it had been her ankle that popped. It wouldn't budge, even though in theory, it should be parallel with the opening and slide right out. She leaned over to move the log behind her by hand in order to fit her foot out of the gap. Her lower back screamed for the awkward reach and bad lifting job. But it was the only angle that would work. She pushed one end of a small log so it stacked on top of another. It was enough space to carefully lift her foot out. She sat on the last log and watched blood rivering out of the long cut.

Taryn tried to slow her breathing again, but couldn't slow the sobs. Couldn't even think about whatever was on the other side of the river. The ankle would make walking impossible, but the bleeding from the cut was what had her really worried. She had to bandage it. Her brain spun as she tried to think rational thoughts. Why hadn't she made better preparations for this hike? A first-aid kit, for example. Even for an easy out and back.

Easy out and back, my ass.

She could use her shirt. Yes, maybe tear a strip off the bottom. She bit into the breathable fabric of her tank top and pulled a section off the shirt. She wrapped it around the deepest part of the cut, but the fabric was too thin. A bit too breathable, it turned out. It wouldn't be enough. The blood would soak through well before any clotting could happen. She sucked air between her teeth. Did she have anything else in the small bag she brought? Yes! The pad. Finally a reason to praise her crazy-ass cycle.

She wanted to cry all over again, but it was relief this time. How lucky that she had a pad with her! Little win.

Taryn removed the strip of tank top. It was already drenched. She took off the bag, felt around the bottom. She peeled open the wrapper and lined the pad up against the deepest part of the cut like a cross. That was where the worst of the wound was located. Plus, she could tie the pad in place around her leg with the bloody strip of fabric. But no, that wouldn't work. There was so much cut still exposed lengthwise. It was bleeding too, much more than she initially thought. What else could she use?

It'd have to be her whole shirt. She pulled her tank top off and lined the pad up vertically with the cut instead. Then she wrapped the whole shirt over her calf and shin, spreading the fabric out in a sort of tight hammock around the wound. She tied a tight knot at the front. It wasn't perfect, but the bleeding wasn't coming through either.

A howl echoed through the canyon. Then another joined in. Wolves. Those were the wolves. No way to tell how close they were, but she had to get moving.

Taryn shimmied down the short distance from the last log to the trail. Her good foot found dirt. She set her hurt leg down and screamed in pain again. Forget walking. Taryn would have to hop. Her ankle couldn't handle even a breeze of pressure coming up through the foot. It must be broken.

Now would be the time for those trekking poles she always wanted Gemma to buy. She needed a nice, long stick to use as a staff. It wouldn't work as well as a crutch, but better than nothing. Taryn turned around and crouched carefully to see underneath the downed logs, keeping her wounded leg extended in sort of a lunge position. It seared like liquid fire and she started to yell out, but stopped herself. It wasn't the time to draw attention.

Sure enough, the spike of the branch that had torn up her leg was loose under there and within reach. She pulled it out and found that it would do, even if it was covered in her blood.

At least the trail was downhill. Breath went out of her and she felt like crying again. What if she slipped and hurt her leg even more? What if she hurt her other leg and couldn't walk at all? How would she escape wolves if it came to that?

Taryn hopped carefully, testing out how it felt to land. To see if she was at risk of slipping. She was moving slower than walking pace, and while not in the worst shape of her life, she definitely felt her forty-plus-years and all the sitting and crying she'd done recently.

Now more than ever before, she had to keep her shit together. Freaking the fuck out was not an option.

She peeled back the pad slightly to see how drenched it was. Red mostly, but there was still some white present around the edges. It didn't seem like blood loss was a major worry. The pad was containing it so far. Then again, blood was mostly water, so losing even a bit of it didn't help the hydration situation. What about an infection? How long would something like that take to set in?

Two miles. She only had two fucking miles to go. And she knew where she was going. It'd take her a whole hell of a lot longer at this pace, but at least she wasn't lost in the middle of the wilderness.

Might as well be at the rate I'm going.

"No, don't think like that," she said to herself. She had to keep the positivity flowing.

Taryn looked up at the sun and judged that it might be close to three p.m. It didn't get cold until dark and it wouldn't get dark until a little after eight. Five hours. She had five hours to make it back to camp. Back to the phone. To get away from whatever was stalking her out there. She just had to keep her head and not fall again. Keep the bleeding under control. And if those things stayed in check, no matter how bad the odds were, she had a chance.

CHAPTER 8

Taryn had walked into the doctor's office that October morning two years prior determined to be a goddamn soldier about whatever news they received. She would be strong for Gemma, the way Gemma had always been for her. But on the drive home, her resolve melted, escaping her body in the form of tears. She shook, unable to hide it.

"Want me to drive?" Gemma had asked, noticing Taryn's struggle. Her voice soft, nurturing, despite that it was her bad news. Her life that was doomed.

"No. We're almost home," Taryn replied, clearing her throat. She had to pull it together. Last thing Gemma needed was Taryn crying on her shoulder.

Dense silence sat between them the rest of the drive. The longer it lingered, the more Taryn wanted to say something to rupture it. And yet, it didn't feel right to do so. Gemma looked out her window and Taryn wondered if she was crying. She had every right to tears.

Taryn blinked her own tears away so she could see to drive. Once they were pulling into the garage, she rallied and spoke. "We'll face this together, like everything else."

Gemma didn't acknowledge the statement right away. She'd unclipped her seat belt and moved to open the door. She walked into the house. Taryn followed, hung car keys on the hook. They both removed their shoes, planted socked feet on hardwood. Taryn's words hung. Expanded into something so large that she felt the fear crawling around inside of them. Did Gemma sense her fear too? It had been a sincere statement, but without any guarantee that things would turn out differently than what the doctor had said. Taryn was desperate to make promises to Gemma. That the doctor was full of shit and what did he know? She wanted to offer the hope of a miracle. Some incantation they could spout to God and in return, receive an extension of Gemma's life. But her words felt thin, cheap. She couldn't force herself to say any of it.

Gemma walked past her, through the kitchen, toward the living room. Taryn was grateful for a few minutes to gather herself, banish tears under the pretense of making a pot of coffee.

Once alone, another emotion thickened the layers of Taryn's fear and sorrow. Guilt. That old familiar pressure. It closed strong hands around her throat, constricting her breath slowly, as if savoring the process of Taryn's suffering. She took a deep breath, held it, released it. She did this until she swallowed down the choking sensation.

Taryn walked into the living room with two mugs of coffee in hand.

Gemma was spinning her wedding ring, staring out the window. Her eyes were wet and she chewed the inside corner of her bottom lip, so it puckered under slightly. She only did that when she was stressed. Of course she was stressed.

Taryn's eyes went to the ring. How the fingers spinning it trembled. The way the tip of Gemma's ring finger was cradled inside the cup of her right hand. Safe. Except nothing about this moment felt safe.

Gemma didn't make eye contact as she spoke. She worked the ring faster. "I've already been through it. You're forgetting that part," she said, answering Taryn's comment from what felt like a lifetime ago.

The words landed like a blow to Taryn. They were a little window of insight into her wife's mindset. Gemma's mother had received the same diagnosis around her age. She had deteriorated over a couple years until all that was left was a shell, a pod of the woman Gemma had known and loved. Her mind had slid into the void until she didn't know who Gemma was, some days didn't really know who she was herself. Early onset Alzheimer's. Very rare, but it ran in families.

Taryn set the two mugs on the coffee table in front of them and stared at the steam rising. She leaned forward, resting her elbows on bent knees. It felt like Gemma was preparing her. Trying to ease into the truth that would crush Taryn.

When Gemma had pushed him hard enough, the doctor admitted there were a couple options. One that most people took, and a second that was rather extreme. Assisted suicide, requiring a trip overseas. Most people didn't choose it because you had to do it while you were still in your right mind, legally speaking. Well before the disease had bored holes into your memories, your personality. While you still had life to live, so to speak. Taryn had wanted to leap across the room and clamp a hand over his mouth. Shut him up. Sitting next to her wife, she could feel Gemma's soul lift with a spark of hope as he discussed it, and Taryn's rage boiled.

Taryn adjusted her position on their couch at home. Swallowed, wiped under her eyes with a quick finger and hoped her long, dark curls would hide the evidence of her tears. A privacy curtain.

Gemma's hand warmed Taryn's knee. Her face was more earnest than Taryn ever remembered seeing it. She knew for sure Gemma was not joking around right now. "I had to watch my father go through it with her. I won't do that to you."

But what about what I want? The words scratched around in Taryn's mouth, dragging long nails along the soft insides of her cheeks. They begged for release, but Taryn didn't dare. She couldn't elevate her own involvement, shouldn't even be thinking about herself right then. But there in the stretch of silence, it all cascaded. One thought, feeling, fear, on top of another.

Fresh ones gathering strength before the previous had any time to resolve.

There was no resolving. That was the bald truth. It was Gemma's decision. She had no say, not least of which because Gemma had followed along in *Taryn's life*. Now Taryn had no claim to try and sway Gemma from making this last choice for herself.

Taryn wanted to follow along and be that person for Gemma, even if she made the unconscionable choice. But it was so much higher a price for Taryn to pay. At least Gemma accepting suburban life still meant they could be together, which was what mattered. What Gemma was asking of Taryn was nothing like that. She was asking her to smile and go along with Gemma's choice to die. Taryn couldn't. It felt wrong. It *was* wrong. It felt like giving up.

CHAPTER 9

Every step is undiluted pain. Pain concentrate. Like juice concentrate. An icy cranberry clump that goes thud in the plastic pitcher. It seeps along the bottom, strings of red fleeing the glob. So red. So angry. Wanting to get away. Be something else. It's coming. Your change. It's almost here. Relief when the kitchen faucet splashes water. A release valve for blood.

Taryn shook her head so hard that her ponytail whipped her cheeks. Why was she thinking about juice right then? She had to stay focused on hopping. One jump and then another. Even though it hurt. Her mind wandered so much. It seemed like she wasn't losing enough blood to pass out, but she didn't know for sure. It felt like something Gemma might have told her over the years, but she couldn't pull it up. Taryn had mostly tuned Gemma out when she shared the details of whatever she uncovered from hours of researching wilderness survival. Only listened with interest to one factoid for every ten Gemma had told her.

Taryn had teased her that she was only a blink away from going full-on prepper. But Gemma's interest wasn't a conspiratorial flex. It was strictly practical. Knowing how to survive, even thrive, in the wild. Because she loved it.

The muscles in Taryn's strong leg were on fire with the additional load it bore in order to baby the bad leg. The downhill didn't help either. She had to go slower, hops turned to little shuffles.

Taryn kept looking across the river, sending her eyes back and forth. Water, rocks, weeds, sagebrush, pine. That was all she saw. Still, no way she wanted to cross the river to the pretty side now. No way she could anyway.

A whimper of a laugh escaped from her. She'd actually kept herself safe from that thing by staying on the creepy side. How's that for survival instincts?

And what *was* that thing?

That shadow.

She didn't want to conjure the image in her mind, but it came anyway. What could be a shadow, but also be solid? It wasn't possible. It was either a shadow or it was solid.

Still, something had been slinking out from behind the pine tree. It moved too briskly to be a cloud covering the sun to create shade. It *was* a shadow. She hadn't made it up.

Maybe she should just think about juice again, because this wasn't helping. Her thoughts about the shadow would only make her heart beat faster, like shoveling coals into a hot oven. Forcing the blood to push harder to get through the escape hatch of the cut in her leg. Make her weaker.

But no, she did remember Gemma talking about this. How the fight or flight response helped the blood to clot.

"Right?" Taryn said out loud, then waited for Gemma in her mind to reply, but there was nothing.

It was right. Her cut would eventually stop bleeding and no amount of stress would inspire a fresh burst of blood. A miniscule flash of hope went through Taryn.

She wanted to take a break, check the cut, but she couldn't afford any unnecessary stops. There was a boulder off to the side of the trail ahead and she'd rest there if she needed to. Assess her wound. Gather her thoughts. It was about twenty feet away. How far had she come? Her vision bobbed as she looked behind while hopping. The log overpass that had given her the wound was right there. Like she'd only taken ten steps. It had been more than ten steps, but not enough. She had hoped the logs would be far out of sight when she checked. Proof that she'd come a long way.

Just then, a thump came up from the ground on the other side of the river. Stronger than a footfall. Much stronger. So loud she heard it over the crash of river. Then a high-pitched yelp, like when you accidentally step on a dog.

She stopped hobbling. At least the cry was recognizable. It had to be a wolf. The other thing? The thump? Not so much. Her brain went ballistic trying to categorize it. She couldn't. It sounded like someone had dropped a sledgehammer on the trail. A single, loud pound. And she couldn't see anything.

She had to get to that boulder up ahead. Hide. She pushed her leg to jump faster. Might as well be a sprint as far as her heart rate was concerned. Pain shot up from her leg into her core, reminding her with every other step downhill that two miles might as well be fifty.

Blood had soaked her sock from the initial cut, hardening at the edges. Sweat soaked her sports bra, gathering at the band.

Push, Taryn. Keep going.

It was like trying to run a six-minute mile for high school soccer tryouts. It had killed her, but she did it. Taryn focused on this, thought about finding a second wind, no pain no gain, and all the other bullshit they told you in sports to make you obliterate your body in the effort. But that pounding noise echoed inside her still. All she could do was get to that boulder.

Push.

The downhill aided in her momentum, although this was precisely how she hurt her leg in the first place, too much momentum. Losing control.

She arrived at the boulder and squatted, extending her hurt leg so as not to aggravate it. It didn't work and she winced, tried not to howl in pain. Her foot was off-kilter, and that made her want to retch. Instead, she thought about the noise again. The thump. What had it been?

Sometimes two trees get caught together by the branches at the tops and when the wind breaks them loose, it snaps back at the base. Like a rubber band, Gemma said as adrenaline banged around inside Taryn.

"It's not two trees, goddammit," she whispered. "There's something over there. I saw it earlier."

But what had she seen? Whatever it was hadn't stuck around. And maybe it was what it looked like—a shadow moving, a deer perhaps. But no, it had more substance than a shadow. And it was so much taller than any deer.

"The Sawtooth has a snout, no eyes—"

"I swear to God, Gem, if you don't shut up, I'll ice you out for a month," Taryn had said when it became clear Gemma would not respect her request to stop talking about the scary Sawtooth all those years ago.

Gemma had laughed.

"I'm serious. No kissing, hugging, nothing. No contact. A month."

"A month, huh?"

"Yep."

Gemma had cocked her head to the side, calculating. "Considering we easily go a month without, the risk feels worth it."

"God, as if 'teeth like a saw and no eyes' aren't already over the line."

"You're so cute when you're worked up," Gemma had slapped Taryn's rear playfully and then continued, pushing words out quickly before Taryn could stop her. "The Sawtooth is like a shark. Only attracted to the scent of blood. Long as you're not bleeding, long as any wounds are covered up, you're fine."

"Fuck," Taryn said now, looking at her bandaged leg. It wasn't bleeding through, but there was definitely blood. Maybe she could remove the bandage and pour water over it, get rid of the blood. She peeked under the pad but couldn't confirm scabbing. She needed to keep it on for now. It would be worse to remove the pad before there was a scab. When she stood back up, her body felt heavy, her mind light.

Was she really entertaining Gemma's story about this Sawtooth creature? It was more likely that she'd seen a funny shadow on the other mountain, not some monster.

Even more likely that it was a wolf, all things being equal. Especially since she'd heard wolves today too. If she were going to choose what to be scared of, better to be scared of an actual animal than some fucking *thing*. But now she remembered something else the biologists had said that night. Wolves didn't stalk humans.

"Wolves are wary of humans, and statistically are the least likely to attack," the biologist had said. "They're social creatures. Did you know the gray wolf can cover up to a hundred miles in a day? I like to think they're eager to get home to the pack at the end of a hunting trip. They like being together." The biologist had stopped to smile, or wait for Gemma and Taryn to agree. They didn't respond at all. "Anyway, being social, they like to communicate, and sometimes that comes out as growling if they're trying to say 'hey, it's my turn to eat this, back off' to another wolf. Or they may howl. People read this as proof of a violent nature, but it's just how wolves talk." She'd handed Taryn an empty plastic lighter fluid bottle. It was punctured with hundreds of tiny holes.

"This is a pup's chew toy," she went on. "They like to play, and often the adult males will join in and wrestle the pups."

Wolves traveled in packs. Rarely solitary. They were social. The howl at the lake could certainly have been a wolf. The other howl too. Those sounded canine. The yelp could have been a wolf. The rockslide at the lake could have been caused by a wolf. Hell, the bones in the water could have been the result of wolves. But wolves didn't stalk people like in the movies.

Whatever was on the other side of the river, whatever had been hiding behind the tree, it wasn't a goddamn wolf.

CHAPTER 10

If only Taryn could stay behind the boulder, hidden until she could be sure whatever made that noise was gone. She held still, strained to listen. But she had to get to camp, even if that meant being exposed again. The thought of it made her want to vomit.

Taryn waited. Heard nothing.

Finally, she had waited long enough. Even if she didn't want to go, she had to. Otherwise, Taryn would sit here until she lost daylight. Then she'd end up trying to find her way back to camp in the dark. There was no other option, she had to push herself forward again. But moving along the trail was so difficult. She needed a splint. It would help the pain if her foot wasn't tugging on the hurt ankle with every hop. Why hadn't she done that already?

There was nothing nearby, no branches at all to use for a splint. Taryn strained to see the trail ahead. In the distance, there was a large, dead tree stump still attached to the ground. It must have fallen at some point, its height broken off. It looked like a vertical shelter. If she could make it there, she'd take another break and reassess again. Surely there'd be wood to make a splint. She could use the backpack to tie it. Or something. She'd figure that out later.

Pulling herself up while only using one leg was hard work and now that she'd stopped for so long, her whole body felt stiff. Pain racked hard, but she sang softly. Distracted herself from it.

She was good at distracting herself from pain. It was how she'd gotten back to work the Monday after Gemma's service. Her coworkers had played along, acting like nothing had happened, just another Monday at the office to bitch about. At least being at her desk didn't remind her of Gemma at every turn. Not like being at home did.

Taryn had grown to hate home since Gemma died. Like biting into a strawberry only to taste the earthy, dead flavor of mold. The home that Gemma never wanted, but Taryn had pushed for. A symbol of her guilt. Her loss.

A cry ripped through the air. That same one, with a quality of vocal layers that a single person couldn't produce. It was audible even over the rush of river, and much louder than the wolf's howling had been.

She pushed herself to go faster while looking behind. Her good thigh screamed threats that it would quit on her.

Don't look back, it'll slow you down, Gemma said.

Right. Taryn kept her eyes facing ahead, even though she longed to peek behind, stand guard for herself as she ran. The tree stump was just thirty feet or so away. She couldn't make her body move any faster. Her good leg hopped and she put weight on the stick in her hand. It wasn't as effective as a crutch, since it only came up to her hip. More like a cane without a handle. Still, she leaned into it, trusting it to redeem itself for causing the cut, and get her to safety.

She stared at the tree trunk, inching closer with every breath. She willed it to uproot and come nearer to her.

Then a shadow appeared behind the tree.

Taryn stopped in the middle of the trail, tried to squint against the sun to see the trunk better. Was it the tree's shadow or something else?

You're spooking yourself again, Gemma said.

"The tree's shadow," Taryn whispered in an exhale. It was thin, filmy like a shadow should be.

She moved her good leg forward and the muscle throbbed with pain again, scolding her for teasing it with a stop. She was almost there, almost to the dead husk of a pine tree where the exposed roots burrowed into scree.

The peculiar scream came again. A bit closer this time, still behind her. Upriver. Loud. So, so loud.

She wanted to yell back at it, like a battle cry. Her fear and frustration with her snail's pace pent up, and now it clamored to get out. But no, she had to focus. Couldn't draw attention.

Her field of vision jumbled with each difficult hop, making the tree dance ahead. Taryn's breathing came hard, and the hammering of blood inside veins echoed loud in her head.

The tree seemed like an oasis, a haven that would tuck her away from danger. A safety zone. If only she could get there. But she was moving so goddamn slow.

Go, go, go. You can do it! as if cheering herself on would actually produce more speed.

Another cry split the air.

Taryn's heart rattled inside its cage, like it was going to break out and run ahead without her slow body.

One...foot...in...front...of...the...oth...er. Taryn repeated this over and over in her mind as she hopped.

She tried to figure out what that sound could be, pin it on something natural, like an animal she'd simply never heard howling before. She didn't hike as often as Gemma, came along maybe five or six times a year, but even so, she'd never heard anything make this sound.

Taryn was almost there, could dive like it was home plate in a softball game if not for her injury.

She touched the safety of rotting bark with a scraped palm that stung from white-knuckling the stick so long. She tucked the walking stick under her armpit to clamp it in a hold. Then, hopping up on the mountainside, off the trail, she leaned into the tree. Its strength braced her bad side, and she circled around to hide inside what used to be solid pine. Her good leg slipped in the effort, and she fell on her hip. She cried but kept moving, pulling herself to sitting in a pile of tree shavings insects had left behind.

Hobbling on one leg would be harder now that her hip had struck rock. It throbbed. *Problem for later.* Right now,

Taryn was cozy, sheltered perfectly inside rot. Her back was against the tree, against the river. Her face pointed up at the dry mountain's incline. It was like a little pocket.

Or a coffin.

She tried to slow her breath, make herself smaller, quieter. Tried not to think about the pain in her leg and now on the other side too, her hip. It almost felt like she could black out from the pain. She was keeping her senses, but how long would that last? Were there insects crawling all over the wood behind her? Crawling all over her backpack, her skin? She brushed off her shoulders, ran a hand along the length of her curly ponytail to be sure nothing had jumped on board there. No bugs. Just her imagination creating worst-case scenarios again.

It felt good to sit. To stop moving. She looked up at the sky, leaned her head against the tree and released a huge sigh. If only Gemma could see her now. No way Taryn ever would have believed she could do this. That she could even hold it together in a situation like this. Especially without Gemma. She smiled, felt the heat of fresh tears. She'd just sit there a quick minute. Not long. Definitely not long. But she deserved a little rest. A reward.

Don't fall asleep, Gemma said. *You need to stay awake, alert. Keep moving.*

Obviously. Taryn wouldn't fall asleep. Just wanted to catch her breath. Feel her heart slow to baseline as adrenaline crashed.

The water coursed, slapping against itself over rocks. It sounded like vague applause.

"The river's cheering me on, Gem," Taryn mumbled, then closed her eyes.

CHAPTER 11

"James Joyce Carol Oates in the Water. Ben Howard's End of the World. I feel fine. Baba O'Riley Killing Kennedy. Dead Kennedys. Killing Lincoln. Rick Grimes. Zombie, zombie, zombieeee," Gemma had said, then fist pumped into the air, and took a bow.

"Explain 'I feel fine' and 'Baba O'Riley,'" Taryn had said.

"End of the world and Teenage Wasteland."

"A wasteland isn't the end of the world."

"But the end of the world is *probably* a wasteland, ya?"

"Nobody knows."

"You're just saying that because this is the best one I've ever done and I'm going to beat you."

"It's pretty good, but game rules state there has to be an obvious connection."

"Fuck the rules in general. I just created pure art. But also, game rules don't state 'obvious.' Just a connection, which there is to me."

"But if it only mattered that the connection was to us personally, we could just say anything—"

"—John Hughes."

"What?"

"*Say Anything*. John Hughes directed it."

"John Hughes didn't do that one. It was Cameron Crowe."

"No way. That was John Hughes."

"Cameron Crowe. Ask Google."

"*Titanic. Avatar*," Gemma said manically.

"God, Gem. You're just pushing my buttons now. Plus, you're still wrong. Those were James Cameron. Your connections have to make sense. You can't just make shit up."

"Look, just give me the win, ok? You invented the game, you're the pop culture and entertainment expert. And you always win. I did good for the first time ever."

Taryn softened.

"Well, I suppose I can see why you thought John Hughes directed *Say Anything*. It definitely has the Hughes vibe, but REM and The Who feel a lot looser. I guess I'll let it slide this time."

Taryn stirred, not fully awake yet. The fuzziness of sleep tried to pull her back down. She didn't want to open her eyes. Craved the oblivion of sleep again so she could keep dreaming of Gemma's weird logic. Of Gemma's laugh and her celebration dances. It was the same logic that got Taryn here in the first place. Why be buried in a cemetery when you could be scattered in the mountains?

The mountains.

Taryn's eyes opened to a blurry blue tint all around. The brightness of day was dimmed in preparation for night. It wasn't dark, not yet, but it would be soon.

"Fuck!" she said, fully awake now. How could she have fallen asleep? She pulled herself toward standing. Too fast. Pain had nested into her good leg, and she moaned. She was dizzy and squeezed her eyes shut, touched her forehead with a soft palm, like she was trying to calm what Gemma called a *speed burn*. What normal people called an ice cream headache.

What time was it? She looked up at the sky, but the sun was behind the mountains. Not officially set, since the jagged peaks tucked it away earlier than true sundown. But the blaze of light and heat was out of sight all the same.

Her ankle was swollen. The splint! She could try and splint it. There would be no movement without something to support that ankle.

She looked around for a piece of wood, but it was all just shavings, chunks of tree too small to use. Frustration flooded inside, pinched at her nose, threatened tears. But there was no room for it. She couldn't get angry right now. Had to stay on task. She moved into a sitting position and tried not to scream as the sting and throb of her lower half sang out. She finally landed fingers on something that might work. It was short and fat enough. It'd have to do.

Taryn removed her backpack and unzipped it. Inside were the filter and water bottle. She pulled them out.

Before she could talk herself out of it, Taryn tossed the filter off to the side. Not too far. She could walk over to it in ten steps. That is, if she could walk. But she didn't need to pack that thing around anymore. It was useless. She held the water bottle, stared at it. How in the world would she carry it if she was going to use the backpack on her leg to hold the stick in a splint?

But she couldn't leave it behind. It was water. How stupid would it be to leave water behind in a situation where you could die of dehydration? Even if it was contaminated water.

Taryn set it down and got to work affixing the stick to the side of her ankle. Two sticks would be better, but she was really woozy now and couldn't go looking for another.

She used the straps of the empty backpack to wrap up the splint and tie it off. She checked her cut. It didn't seem like her leg was still bleeding, but what would happen when she started moving again?

The river was loud static in her mind now. A station on an old TV set that she couldn't turn off. She wanted to scream at it to shut up and let her think, but her brain moved slowly, like cold syrup. She had to get moving. Easy hops on the trail, one after another. But how would she hop with her hip feeling like it might buckle under pressure?

Then the thirst tore through. Taryn had never known what it meant to be thirsty before this moment. She felt the back of her neck. Sandy, like she'd laid down on a beach. She rubbed fingers together and then tasted the coarse granules with a dry tongue. Salt from her sweat.

Dying of thirst while listening to a river burble. Nice. How funny that her main concern a few hours ago had been being slightly parched on the hike back. Now she was facing real dehydration, blood loss, hiking at night, and whatever that thing was that she saw—or didn't see—following her. There were wolves out here which, according to science, didn't stalk people. But this was the same science that gave Gemma only a year or two to live. And a way to die. Taryn was a huge supporter of science, but that didn't mean science was all knowing. There was so much more to learn about the body, the world.

At least Taryn's reasoning skills were returning. Good, good.

The thirst. She had to drink the unfiltered water. Had to.

But it could make her sick.

But how would she continue this way? The thirst was ruthless, gripping, demanding the focus of her mind. Removing her ability to assess anything else. One little sip couldn't make her too sick. Just a sip.

Taryn unscrewed the lid. She smelled the water. It wasn't fishy. Didn't *smell* contaminated. But that was stupid, what did contaminated water smell like? Not like she could sniff out bacteria. Viruses that might be alive inside plastic.

Her self-control was sucked into a vortex of thirst. She could pretend to resist drinking this water, but deep inside, knew it was inevitable. Her mind wouldn't be able to focus on pushing through the pain with this greedy thirst on center stage. It only made sense to deal with that problem.

She took a sip. It tasted fine, so she took a real drink. Then another.

Just because it tastes fine doesn't mean it is, slow down!

With the thirst dulled, she returned the lid and tightened it.

Branches rustled from across the river, punctuating the white noise.

She froze in place, still hidden behind the tree.

There were no branches on her side of the river, so it had to be on the other side.

Taryn waited to hear it again. Wanted to look, but couldn't get her body to move.

James Joyce Carol Oates. James Joyce Carol Oates. James Joyce Carol Oates.

The words did loops in her mind. But she needed to focus, think about what to do next. She used the words to slow down, count four seconds of breath in, then four seconds out.

James Joyce Carol Oates.
In.
James Joyce Carol Oates.
Out.

Branches moving, breaking now.

This time it seemed the sound wasn't directly across the river from her. It was coming from upstream just a bit. But definitely not on her side. She released the breath she'd just taken in.

Still, what had cracked those branches? Taryn had to know for sure. There was still plenty of light to see. She slowly looked around the shell of a tree. A mule deer was drinking in the shallow of river about fifty feet upstream.

Her body deflated as relief poured all the way in.

"Just a deer," she whispered, bracing her weight against the tree to stand without pressure on her ankle. She kept watching, even though her head felt like a helium balloon, craving release into the sky.

Then the brush behind the deer moved.

The deer perked its head, went statuesque as if evaluating the threat. It had an open wound, a red streak across the side of its neck. Something had gotten to it, but apparently not killed it.

Or it ran across a gnarly stick, same as your leg, Gemma said.

The leaves parted, and something emerged slowly, stalking the deer. Taryn thought she saw a round—something. Head maybe? Definitely a protrusion too—a snout. She couldn't make out any other defining features. But these were huge in size.

Taryn pulled her face behind the tree again, but no. She had to see. Had to know.

Leaning out, only exposing enough of herself to watch, Taryn saw it. The shadow was a deep shade of charcoal. Not thin, like the husk of tree shadow had been earlier. More opaque, physical. But it didn't have skin. Certainly not skin, and not hide. It was the shadow she'd seen darting around on the other side earlier in the day. Its actual face had made actual leaves move. True shadows didn't do that. This had substance. Empty substance. That was what came to her in the moment. A stupid oxymoron of a term, but it fit.

In one leap, the shadow was on top of the deer. Outmatching it in size by ten to one. There against the gray depth, its many arms flailed. Jagged teeth emerged, sinking into brown hide. Teeth tore the deer open at the neck in one flick. Blood sprayed upward in an arc like wings. Then the thing released the deer, so that prey landed with a flop on the ground, out of sight.

The shadow turned toward Taryn, like it sensed her. It was looking at her.

But it had no eyes. How could she know where it was looking?

She knew.

Taryn covered her mouth to mask a scream. She pulled herself behind the tree again, out of sight.

Teeth. Jagged, sharp teeth. Like a saw. *Sawtooth.*

She licked dry lips, tried to lay hold of a single thought as a barrage of them came. But the urge to look again, to see the thing that had mowed down a deer in one strike was too strong. She leaned against the tree and peered out over the river again.

Nothing.

There was nothing there. No deer, and certainly no Sawtooth.

CHAPTER 12

"It's not real," Taryn whispered. "Can't be."

But she had seen it. She had been awake, focused, and had seen it as clearly as anything.

It's not helpful to think about the Sawtooth, Gemma said.

But what did she know? This Gemma was just in Taryn's mind. It wasn't Gemma speaking to her at all, it was Taryn speaking to herself. When she was arguing with Gemma, she was actually arguing with herself. Even though Taryn had always known this on some level, the flat realization made her feel more alone, like she'd lost Gemma all over again. As if her entire life would be a process of losing her wife again and again and again. Would it ever end? How could she go on like this?

No matter. If she was going to move forward on the trail, which yes, she absolutely had to do that, it was better if she didn't believe in the Sawtooth. It *was* all in her mind. Gemma's snide comments, encouragement, instructions. All things Taryn remembered or imagined Gemma saying. Same with the Sawtooth. The creature was only in her mind because of what Gemma had said to scare her years ago. It had morphed into some hallucination from the trauma of pain. Or some obsessive thought, based in fear. That's all. She had to get back to camp. Back to the phone, and daylight was racing away.

Taryn moved out from behind the cored-out tree. Her good leg was stiff, sore. She tried to hop, but it buckled. She fell on the ground and her bad foot hit hard dirt, torqued her ankle more. Her water bottle went flying forward on the trail. Taryn cried out in pain, then lay all the way down, on her stomach. Agony surged through her body, made her weak, like she was unable to move even her fingers for fear that her ankle would feel it.

She had so much further to go. It hadn't even been half a mile from the log overpass to the boulder. And again, such a short distance from the boulder to the tree. Those stretches had all but killed her. How much worse off was she now that her hip had quit? Now that she'd hurt her ankle again? Imagining making her way in the dark felt impossible.

No way she could spend the night out here though. What? Just go to sleep on the trail and then take all day to get back to camp tomorrow?

Not with whatever she just saw out there.

She waited for Gemma in her mind to pipe up. She didn't.

The sun was down and it had turned into night while Taryn flitted through thoughts. She moved her face to look up at the sky. Couldn't see the moon from this limited angle, but it was definitely out there. Not bright like it was full, but at least it wasn't a new moon. And these stars! They were glowing. Another win for her to tally.

She had plenty of light to see by. Spending the night out there was stupid. Taryn had to keep moving while she still could.

Pulling herself up into a modified upward dog position, Taryn's elbows dug into the trail. Small rocks protruded like tips of icebergs in the dirt. She'd have to avoid scratching her skin. Last thing she needed was more blood to contend with. Crawling wasn't easy, but she moved further in one motion than she'd done hopping along. Her water bottle was just out of reach.

The elastic waistband of her shorts dragged, slipped down, collected debris like it was working on commission. The trail rubbed along her exposed and tender stomach and thighs. She stopped to make sure none of it broke the skin.

Taryn grasped the water bottle, held it by the plastic loop and slowly moved back onto her stomach. She started the army crawl downhill again.

CHAPTER 13

"Gemma, what do you think about what Taryn just shared?" The therapist's words had been gentle, the room quiet except for Taryn sniffling back tears.

It was their first time in couple's therapy. Gemma had joked about that. *Of course, the only time I need marriage counseling is when I'm almost dead.*

Gemma had cleared her throat, fighting tears. She'd been spinning her wedding ring the entire meeting. Elbows resting gently on knees, touching faded jeans. She shrugged. "I hate that it's hard for her. Obviously. But she has no idea how much harder it would be if I decided to ride this horse into the sunset. I'll still die in the end. The choice isn't die now, or don't die. It's die now, or die later. And die later is full of trauma along the way."

"Do you even realize how many times you said the word, 'die'?" Taryn whispered.

Gemma didn't respond.

The therapist looked at them, her face a blank canvas. Taryn tried to read something into it. Tried to see if she had an opinion on this, but couldn't divine anything.

Gemma turned to look at Taryn on the couch. There were tears. "Babe, I hate this," she said. "I hate that I'm going through it. I hate that you're going through it with me. But I'm not changing my mind."

Taryn didn't reply at first. She stared at Gemma's hands working the ring. Despite that they were shaking, the ring spun, friction growing with each revolution.

When she didn't respond, the therapist asked, "Taryn, did you hear what Gemma said about her decision?"

Taryn gave a single nod, reached for the box of tissue and dabbed her eyes, then wiped the tissue across her nose. "I understand that this is what she wants. It's just that..." she sniffed and cleared her throat, hesitated to say what came next. She'd already been around this mountain with Gemma, already given this very good, very reasonable response so many times, only to have it shot down. "What if Gemma actually has a lot more time than they think? They say a year or two, but what if it's three? Five? Do the doctors really know? They can't predict the future. They're not magicians. They just make educated guesses. There's still room for hope."

"What's a few more years if they're bad years?" Gemma said.

"We all die," Taryn shot back. "Everyone dies. Does that mean we should just give up? Kill ourselves?"

It was harsh, Taryn knew it as the words came out. But she was desperate to change Gemma's mind. Time to pull out the big guns.

"Nice, Tare. I won't respond to that last part. I don't think you mean it. But I will repeat the thing you never seem to hear. I have to do it before I lose my faculties and I don't know when that point will come, so I have to act now. It's not about giving up, it's about dying with dignity. I don't want to die like my mom did. Just a shadow of herself. A helpless, needy thing that has no idea how much of a burden she's become. No clue how easy it is for those who love her the most to teeter into resentment. How they'll hate themselves for it."

Gemma reached for the tissue box too. Taryn had never heard that last part before. Never heard Gemma talk about her mom as a burden. Her mom was already failing by the time Taryn and Gemma were together. Gemma spent a lot of time up in Garden Valley to be with her mom toward the end, but she'd never let on that it was anything other than *what you do when you love someone*. And how many years now had Gemma kept this to herself? Not shared these feelings, this grief with Taryn?

"Is that what you're afraid will happen, Gemma? That you'll become a burden to Taryn?" the therapist said.

"You could never be a burden to me," Taryn said. "I want to take care of you, I—"

"Let Gemma answer, please," the therapist interrupted.

Taryn nodded.

Gemma didn't speak right away, she was crying too hard, and Gemma didn't cry often enough to know how to talk through sobs. It was a skill you had to cultivate. She just sort of started, stopped and swallowed hard. Then mewled a quivering sound until a huge frown overtook her face, and then it was all sniffling and wiping saltwater from her eyes.

They waited.

Taryn wanted to cut in again. Make this better. Reassure Gemma that she had said *in sickness and in health* and she had meant it back then. She still meant it. That she'd make sure Gemma spent her last years doing exactly what she loved. Being in the woods, the mountains, hell, Taryn would buy a place for them to live out there until Gemma's days were done. She owed Gemma those years. They'd live *Gemma's life*. If she could just show Gemma that things wouldn't be the same as they were with her mom. That Taryn *wanted* to spend these next years taking care of Gemma, was choosing it. She'd quit her job. They had plenty of money to live for a while.

Taryn couldn't help it, so she spoke up. "But I—"

The therapist put her hand up to stop her before she could get more than two words out. It felt like being silenced by a teacher. Taryn wedged her hands into her lap and watched the drip of her own tears darken her jeans while she waited.

"Yes," Gemma said. "I know for a fact I'll become a burden. I lived it. Never imagined I'd feel a sense of relief when Mom finally passed away. I loved her more than anything until I met Taryn. I don't want that to happen to us, and it seems like my choice."

"How does it feel that Taryn doesn't see it the same way?" the therapist asked.

Taryn felt the start of a little red alert in her mind. *Danger ahead: They're about to side against you.* Taryn had been in therapy before. Not with Gemma, but by herself, for her own childhood baggage. It always, *always* ended up being about her *control issues*. Never mind that she was a neglected child, raised in poverty. Somehow it always came down to her *need for control*. She even felt at times that something about her personality was triggering to someone who would become a therapist. A bad match, no matter who sat across from her. Taryn had sworn off therapy years ago, after she'd cried to a therapist about growing up alone while her alcoholic mother was out at the bars. That therapist had turned it around to Taryn's control issues, and she had stood up and walked out. Maybe she did have control issues, probably she did. Maybe they even needed to be addressed, but there was a timing issue that therapists just didn't seem to understand. You don't bring that shit up after someone has poured out their soul full of trauma to you. Especially when you're the first person they've ever voiced it to.

"I feel hurt," Gemma said. "And a little angry, even though I don't want to be. But this is my choice, and Tare's only making it harder by pushing back on it instead of supporting me."

"Do you hear Gemma? That she needs your support right now?" the therapist said.

Taryn nodded. "But I can't support her choice when she's choosing to give up completely, not even try."

Gemma had broken down in sobs again.

The therapist looked at Taryn like she was a child in trouble. "Do you think it's your choice, Taryn? How Gemma should proceed with her diagnosis?"

Taryn looked down and shook her head. It wasn't her choice, of course.

The therapist let the silence grow. Only Gemma's sniffling and heaving breaths punctuated it, and so the room filled to suffocation with all the things Taryn wasn't allowed to say. Maybe not even allowed to feel.

CHAPTER 14

Taryn clenched her jaw as she pulled her body along the trail in a crawl. Why hadn't she heard the Sawtooth again? She had to stop thinking about that damn Sawtooth. But she couldn't let her mind focus on the gutting pain that came with every movement forward either.

Don't think about the Sawtooth. Don't think about the pain. Don't think about the darkness. Your thirst, the dead corpse germs swimming inside your gut. Don't think about how you shouldn't be thinking about any of these things.

She wanted to scream in frustration again. Why couldn't she make her mind an ally? Why did she have to fight against *it*, too?

Taryn tried to recall stories of great physical feats. The mom who lifted a car to save her baby. How people could overcome astounding odds, if they stayed mentally tough. But that was a problem. When her mind wasn't needling a litany of worries, it was fuzzy. Stuck in the past. Useless.

Play the game, Gemma said.

"God, where have you been?" Taryn said, but then immediately wondered where the Sawtooth could be. Why had it been so quiet?

Back to thinking about the Sawtooth. *Fuck.* The game it was. If Taryn couldn't keep her lizard brain under control, she'd play the game. Where to start?

Brown-Eyed Girl, Gemma said.

"Brown-Eyed Girl..." Taryn said slowly, taking her time to think, as if Gemma was actually there to call foul on her hesitation to find connections. As if Gemma would actually ever call foul.

"Brown-Eyed Girl, Interrupted. Angelina Jolie... no...Winona Ryder," Taryn brainstormed out loud. It was totally against the rules. You had to say the song, book, movie title, or celebrity name right the first time, no switching. But she couldn't help it. "Not Angelina Jolie. Too hard to follow up on," Taryn mumbled to herself.

"Girl, Interrupted. Winona Ryder…Easy Rider, Riders on the Storm, rider… spider…fighter. Fuck!"

It felt impossible to do when she was in pain, parched, scared. She kept crawling, tried to slow her mind down into focus.

"Winona Ryder. Stranger Things…Fall Apart!" Taryn said, triumphant. Anytime you could squeeze a literary piece in there alongside all the mindless actors and song titles, it felt like a win. But then no, it didn't work. Winona Ryder was already a sentence break. She needed something to piggyback with Ryder in-sentence.

Who cares about sentence breaks? Take it from the top, Gemma said.

"Brown-Eyed Girl, Interrupted. Winona Ryder. Stranger Things Fall Apart…of Your World. We Are the World. The Lost World…War Z… For Zechariah. The Book of Eli…"

Too many breaks. Too many goddamn breaks. She needed continuity. Connection.

"Too many breaks. Can't do it right," she said as if Gemma in her mind needed to hear it spoken out loud.

You made the game up, and you're the only one who ever cared about the rules. So, like I always say, fuck the rules, and keep going, Gemma said.

"I'm tired. It hurts so bad."

No response. Taryn kept crawling. "Fine. Brown-Eyed Girl, Interrupted. Winona Ryder. Stranger Things Fall Apart of Your World. We Are the World. The Lost World War Z for Zechariah. The Book of Eli …Wiesel. Night…of the Living Dead…"

Zombies.

Taryn stopped crawling and pushed out a little laugh. Zombies, of course! It always came back around to death. Almost every time she and Gemma played this game. Gemma thought the game was just a reflection of a person's psychology, where their particular mind went. And death had been on their minds for far too long. But right now, death was the last thing she wanted to—

"FUCK!" Taryn shouted. Her ankle had knocked against one of the larger protruding rocks on the trail. She'd been carefully avoiding them, feeling first with her arms, but it was too dark to see the ones along the outside edges of the trail, and she was too focused on the game.

The pain made her head go floaty. She stopped crawling, laid her head in the dirt and her stomach heaved with nausea. Crying was making it worse. She tried to take deep breaths, but couldn't lift her head away from the dirt. Her lungs drew in particles and they hit her throat. She coughed hard and that made pain seize all over her body. There was warmth all over, then nothing.

CHAPTER 15

When Taryn opened her eyes, it was like flipping on a light switch to find out the bulb was burned out. Still dark. She was on her side, her neck bent, and her back propped up against something cool. She felt along it with fingers. Earth. Was she underground? She tried to sit up, but her head hit a ceiling of dirt, and the motion woke up the pain in her leg. Taryn moaned. She laid back down. Then the putrid smell arrested her, funneled up into her nostrils so she could taste it in her mouth. Her pores absorbed it. Taryn gagged, but nothing came up.

"You awake in there?" a voice from the outside said. Deep, like a man.

What the hell? Someone's out there? She couldn't see anyone. Taryn worked toward movement again, was zinged by intense pain again, laid down again.

She felt around in the dark from her side position. Her hand touched something soft. Fur. Squishy, wet. She pulled her hand away and didn't have to smell it to know it was exactly where the stink came from. There was a dead animal down there. Was she in a wolf den? Her eyes adjusted a bit, and against the traces of moonlight, she saw three tiny animal bodies next to her in this cramped, underground space. The river was muffled, but she could hear it. It was still night out, but faint light came in from above.

"Where am I?" Taryn asked.

"One of the Sawtooth pack's dens."

Dead wolf pups. She had been right. Oh God, how did she get here?

"Been waiting for you to wake up." The man's voice was raspy.

"Who are you? Why am I here?"

"Name's Craig, and you're here because *it* brought you here, same as me. But that's better than what it did to Rachel. That thing tie you up too?"

It? That thing?

"No, I don't think so. Not my hands at least," she said, moving them again to confirm even though she didn't need to. She couldn't move her feet at all.

"Thought as much. When it shoved you down in that den, you weren't bound. Gave me some hope. Can you crawl out of there?"

The opening was on a slight incline and it was very small. She was definitely underground. But somehow, she'd gotten in. Craig had said it *shoved* her in. So many thoughts were vying for attention, the loudest right now was why had the Sawtooth put her in the den instead of devouring her like the deer? No answers came, so she focused on moving her torso toward the opening. Taryn cried out in pain.

"Be quiet. It might hear," Craig said.

"I'm too injured to move."

"You have to try. Go slowly."

"The pain is too much, I'm afraid I'll pass out again." But even saying it, she knew Craig was right. She had to try.

"Here, I'll talk while you work on it. Keep you distracted, get you up to speed on my plan. Then we can get the hell out of here once you climb out. What's your name?"

"Taryn."

"All right, Taryn. I'm Craig, like I said. I'm a grad student studying the Sawtooth pack, and I'm sure you've found the pups by now." Craig released a sigh of disgust. "What a waste. Those pups were so young. They don't live long in the wild anyway, you know. Five, six years if they're lucky. Anyway, Rachel and I were just across the river from here. That's where we set up a satellite camp…"

Taryn tried to listen but it took a lot of concentration to inch her way over the wolf pup carcasses without bathing herself in gore.

"We'd been here four days when we ran across that thing. We were packing up to head down the river to basecamp when we heard it. God, if only I hadn't listened to Rachel. I wanted to leave the day prior, but she had to get more goddamn data. Never enough data for Rachel. Anyway, at first, we didn't think much of the cry. Wasn't a wolf, but it sounded so far away that we shrugged it off— How you doing? Making any progress?" Craig interrupted himself.

"All right, just trying to get past these poor creatures."

"Good. So, then this afternoon, that thing was in our camp. In broad daylight, just this shadow pacing around. It got to Rachel first. I heard a struggle, her screaming..." Craig paused here, like he was trying not to cry. "So, I ran to see. When I got close, she was lying on the ground, that thing had torn into her stomach. It was eating her, but she was still alive. She was still fucking alive, motioning for me to run, to get away. Everything was going so slow and I couldn't decide what to do. I just stayed there. Then it grabbed me, tied me up, and everything went black. I woke up here, hands and feet bound."

The cry. The shadow. It was the Sawtooth.

"It's been following me, but never close enough to attack," Taryn grunted, now over the pup carcasses. She pulled her full weight on to her arms, trying to army crawl toward the incline that led to the den opening, presumably where Craig was located.

"What are you doing out here? No trails in this area."

"I was hiking up to the alpine lake."

"No idea where that is. Like I said, no hiking trails anywhere around here."

Talking made Taryn lose track of the pain momentarily, so she continued as she pushed elbow over elbow, starting up the incline now.

"I saw bones in the lake," Taryn said. "Do you think the wolves did that?"

Why did it matter? It didn't, not really. But she was trying to think of things to say and it was what came out.

"Could have. But I doubt they dragged the bones into the lake. Wolves like fresh meat and rarely clean a carcass completely," he paused, like he was considering it. "Although, they do leave their kills lying around after the pack has fed. Scavengers, even bears, will adopt the carcass. Who knows where a bear could drag a dead animal."

"Or a human," Taryn said. "One of the bones looked like a femur."

"No, not a human." Craig was defensive. "These wolves don't hunt people. That's a myth, a misconception."

Taryn changed the subject, uninterested in debating about it. "You said you have a plan."

"Yeah. You cut me loose and then we make a break for the river. It's super shallow here. We used to come to this spot for observation because the wolves used it as a drinking fountain. Easy crossing. Then we get into the canoe, just down the bank on the other side, and paddle back to basecamp. It's just the getting untied part that I haven't been able to get past."

Taryn was almost there, almost to the opening. She could feel the fresh air blowing on her cheeks.

"Why did it tie you up instead of attacking you?" she asked.

"No clue. It seemed out of sorts after it got Rachel, almost drunk-like. It struggled with coordination as it tied me up. I tried to fight, but it was still too strong."

When Taryn's face broke above ground, the air was chilly, the stars gleaming, and Craig was bound, hands and feet next to a tree. It was a tree similar to the one she'd hidden in earlier, but still alive. It had an exposed root system, which provided cover for the wolf den. He was just a few feet away.

Taryn grunted, birthing herself from the small opening. She looked all around now that she was free of the den. It was dawn, faint traces of light pushed against the mountains. The river ran below about twenty feet, closer than she'd been to it all day. It was calm, smooth, with only a trickling noise. No mad rush of white caps.

"There you are. Okay, get me loose," Craig said.

"Do you have a knife?"

"Of course not. Don't you think if I had a knife, I'd have used it?"

"I just thought maybe you had one out of reach or something."

Taryn made her way to his hands, felt that it wasn't just rope, it was paracord. Her heart sunk. Without a knife, paracord would be impossible to break. She went to loosen the knots. They were tied so tightly that she couldn't get a grip on the small bulges. That's when she felt Craig's bracelet.

"You have a survival bracelet on."

"Yeah, big deal. More paracord."

Taryn chuckled to herself. God, if only Gemma could see her now. She unfastened the clip of his bracelet and wiggled it out from under the bonds. This created a tiny bit of slack. Not enough that Craig could pull his hands out, but she didn't need that much. She worked to pull apart Craig's bracelet.

"What the fuck? What are you doing?"

"I can use it to cut the cord."

"What?"

"Yep. My wife taught me how to do it," Taryn spoke as she unraveled the bracelet into one single cord. "Pretty much the only one of her survival hacks I paid attention to because I didn't believe it could be done. Made her prove it."

A loud cry cut through the night. Taryn's breath hitched in her throat. The white glow of Craig's eyes grew rounder. Then the Sawtooth roared again with what sounded like a thousand voices.

"Hurry!" he said.

The paracord around Craig's wrists was wrapped three times. She pulled on one strand tightly to create a little hump of slack.

"Ouch," he said.

"Sorry." She pushed one end of his bracelet cord under the slack cord. It made a sort of cross.

"This might burn a little."

"I don't care. Do it!"

"Lean back as I pull. There has to be a lot of resistance."

Craig stiffened to brace himself.

Taryn worked the bracelet paracord against the cord binding Craig's hands. Back and forth in a sawing motion, as fast as she could manage, keeping the friction on the same spot. She felt dizzy, it was a lot of exertion in her state.

Craig sucked his teeth in pain.

"Doesn't take long, hang in there," Taryn said, sawing. "That animal's called a Sawtooth. My wife's uncle saw it once."

"It's no animal. Please hurry."

The cord snapped and Craig's hands were free. He took the bracelet cord from her and tried to push it under a loop around his ankles to free his feet. His hands were shaking. Taryn saw the other side of his face now. It was drenched in blood.

The Sawtooth is like a shark attracted to blood.

Her leg. His face.

Another piercing cry through the night.

In the space of nanoseconds, a few realities coalesced in Taryn's mind. Thoughts clearer than anything she'd had in hours.

The Sawtooth was coming.

They couldn't outrun it. They had to hide.

Hiding was only possible if the creature couldn't sense blood.

They had to get into the river to wash the blood off. It was their only chance.

Just then, branches jostled from further up the mountain, behind them.

CHAPTER 16

Taryn turned to look, but saw only the slight sway of a low bush, leftovers from movement.

Craig was struggling to get the cord in place to free his feet.

"Let me do it," she said, taking the bracelet cord from Craig's shaking hands. He had almost gotten it under one of the loops around his ankles, but he was too slow.

He nodded, looking behind, in the direction of the brush noise from before. "Hurry."

Taryn sawed back and forth until the cord around his feet snapped.

"Come on, let's go," Craig said, standing, pulling cord away and extending a hand to her.

"Just a sec."

Taryn tore through the tank top and pad on her leg. It didn't seem like her cut was bleeding any more. Another small win. She pushed the bloody top of her sock down into her hiking boot so it was hidden. Wincing in pain as she went. Then she set the bloody maxi pad and all of its trimming to the side, right by the den's opening. Hopefully it, along with the blood on the wolf pups would attract the Sawtooth. Keep it away from the river. Away from them.

"What are you doing? Let's go!" Craig whispered.

She ignored the question.

It had grown quiet behind them. Too quiet.

"Come here," Craig reached down and pulled her to her feet, but she wobbled and stifled a cry. He ignored it, wrapped her arm around his neck. He took steps toward the water and spoke fast, breathless. "There's one fast part in the river. Canoe handles it fine. Just have to…pay attention. Basecamp's where the river bends."

"You have to get that blood off your face the second we reach the water. It's attracted to blood," Taryn said.

Craig nodded, like he already knew that. No way he could.

They moved downhill to the river in a quick shimmy. It was close, maybe ten feet away now. They were going faster than Taryn thought possible. The pain was excruciating, but she tried to relax, let Craig do the work for now.

A howl from just behind them jerked both of their bodies in a startle, Craig kept going. Taryn's feet began to drag, the ground banging against her ankle, making her see blinking star flecks across her vision. She wanted to scream, but she wouldn't. No fucking way. She bit her tongue to force herself into silence.

They were almost to the water. If Taryn was capable of jumping, she could lunge for it.

"Jump. We have to jump in!" Taryn said.

But then, Craig was gone.

She looked over, as if it were slow motion. The Sawtooth overtook him like it had with the deer. She was tossed aside by the force of contact and now they were a foot or two behind her. Craig screamed in terror. The sudden absence of him as her human crutch sent Taryn hurtling forward onto her stomach.

She crawled with every ounce of energy she had left. Fingers touched wet rocks, then submerged into the icy river. The cold knocked all breath out of her. It was early morning now, daylight streaming across the valley, and she crawled further, further into the water until her body was as submerged as she could get it. The water didn't cover her back, but her legs were underneath, her arms, and she put her chin into it, used her hands to splash and wipe water all over her face.

It was cold. She couldn't stay in there. But what if she started bleeding again? Best to stay for now. Think of next steps.

Craig's screams came to a quick halt, so the only noise against the tiny trickle of river was the sound of goring. Taryn looked behind and saw the Sawtooth more clearly. It was tall, various limbs sticking out in no particular pattern. It moved its face against warm, open flesh and intestines. Steam filtered out of Craig's body. The thing was feasting.

The Sawtooth didn't seem to notice her even though it was broad daylight. She was a thousand percent dependent on being hidden because of no blood. This leftover bit of lore Gemma had shared. Had no clue if it would even work, but it was all she had right then.

The Sawtooth's hitching breath was wet, and it gurgled as it took in whole, raw pieces of Craig. Moments passed, although it seemed hours to Taryn. She waited. Tried to ignore the numbness overtaking her legs and arms. Watched the Sawtooth's limbs instead. They wavered, as if in sync together. She counted four legs, at least five arms, maybe more if you included the little stubs coming out of its torso, not quite arms. There were fingers attached to what were certainly hands. Craig was right, it wasn't fully animal, but still so inhuman. That charcoal color made it look like its skin was burned. Suddenly, its arms moved out of control. At times working against each other, one hand taking the spoils out of another. The creature was growing clumsy, sloppy in its movement. Even slowing down.

Then it came to attention, like it heard something. It pointed its snout up into the air. Could it smell her? She swallowed down panic and tears, held still.

No way to tell if it was looking at her. It was just a dark, empty outline, except for those teeth. Although if it saw her, wouldn't it attack? At least tie her up? What would she do if it came toward her?

Before she had time to contingency plan, her worst fear happened. The thing came at her. Bounded so fast on four legs, but didn't get into the water. It felt around the shore with those arms, as if it were blind.

It was like it couldn't see her. Couldn't tell she was there. It was so close she could probably smell its breath if she wasn't holding her own.

Taryn squeezed eyes shut, waiting. Then the Sawtooth turned and went toward the den. It picked up the maxi pad, dropped it.

And then, something really miraculous happened. It slumped down on top of the maxi pad and stopped moving.

Was it asleep? Surely, it wasn't dead. Taryn's luck wasn't anything close to that good. Especially not in the last twenty-four hours.

Taryn waited for a few more moments, until she was sure it was asleep. Then she turned back around to face the other riverbank, the side that held the canoe. She hadn't moved even an inch when a voice came into her mind. But like nothing she'd ever heard before. It wasn't Taryn's brain conjuring up words, not even under the guise of Gemma. No. This was literally an audible voice in her head, echoing loudly as it spoke a single word.

"Taryn."

CHAPTER 17

It was Gemma's voice, but not like before. This was Gemma's actual audible voice ringing through her skull. Taryn stopped moving across the river. She looked all around, but didn't see anything. The Sawtooth was still in a slump by the tree. Was she imagining it? No, she'd heard her wife's voice. She was certain. The sound was like a gong in Taryn's brain. Not so loud to cause pain, but volume enough so Taryn knew it was real.

But if this was Gemma, why couldn't she see her?

"I can't find you, but I need to," Gemma said. "Have to get that ring back."

"You're dead," Taryn whispered finally, afraid of waking the Sawtooth. "I just scattered your ashes at the lake. Are you a ghost?"

Taryn's eyes flashed all around, desperate to make sense of this. But she didn't see a single thing out of the ordinary. Other than the Sawtooth, and it was still a slump of slumber.

"I wish," Gemma said. "But it's a tad worse than that. Now, where are you? I need the ring."

Anger flared inside Taryn. It surprised her. Anger, of all things. Here they were, communicating impossibly, across time and space, life and death, and all Gemma cared about was—the ring? Why? Taryn looked at her finger, at the flash of gold shimmering in the water.

"Why do you care so much about a piece of jewelry when we're here, speaking, together again?" Taryn said, relief overcoming anger as her words polished the truth of this moment. She had Gemma back. "I need your wilderness survival brain. We have to go before that thing wakes up."

Tears came and the heat of saltwater reminded her just how cold her skin was. She looked around again. Where was Gemma?

"I'm not here. Not really, at least. I can't let you leave until you give me the ring. Quick! Before they wake up."

"What? Before who wakes up?" Taryn asked the question in a whisper at the same time her mind answered it. Gemma was talking about the creature. Had to be. But why say *they*?

"The Sawtooth," Gemma said. "I knew you remembered my story when I found that bloody bandage. You must have washed off all your blood. It was the blood that drew them. Tossing that pad away was smart. Super smart to use the pad too, by the way."

What the fuck?

"We need to go," Taryn said. No time to chat. "There's a canoe. Help me get there. Why can't I see you?"

"I only have one shot at getting the ring. That's when you'll see me. I think if I can get rid of it before they're awake enough to realize what's happening, it may work."

"What may work? Who are *they*? Is there more than one of them? You're not making any sense."

Nothing from Gemma at first, and Taryn felt Gemma's hesitation to answer creeping along the line of her neck, inching toward the nape, where it inspired prickles of dread. Something wasn't right. Duh, something wasn't right, Taryn was communicating with the dead in the midst of a life and death struggle with some mythical creature. But there was more, she felt it, but couldn't zero in enough to figure out what it was. The river trickled over tiny stones, a shallow pouring sound that grew loud in the silence. She needed to get out of the water, that was a fact. Had to warm up. Get into the canoe. But her body stayed, her mind posed questions back to her. Why go? What was moving forward worth if Gemma was *here*? Why go back to a life without her?

"It's my mom. Grandma too," Gemma began to answer Taryn's question. "They're the ones I recognize, although Grandma not really. Mom tells me it's her and that's what I'm going from. Mom's almost gone, slipping into the hunger. Says when she first got here, Grandma was in her right mind, but over time, the hunger has consumed her the way it consumed the rest of them."

"The rest of them? So there's more than one?"

"The primordial ones, that's what Mom calls them. No, there's just one Sawtooth. Many souls occupying the same body. Absorbed into the hunger, slowly becoming one with it."

"You're scaring me. What the fuck is the hunger?"

"Babe, I don't have time to explain the ins and outs. I need the ring. That's what's keeping everything together. It's the only way to save you. Please, where are you?"

"Why can't you see me? How come you can hear and speak with me, but not find me? Just follow my voice. Or show yourself so I can come to you."

This was Gemma. No doubt about it. But something about the situation made Taryn hesitate to give away her location.

Gemma let out a little defeated sigh, like she was just now realizing something. "I thought you understood. The blood. It's the only way we can navigate, see anything, really. We're blind. And sound is a sphere all around, an endless echo coming from everywhere and nowhere at the same time. Blood is a point on a map."

A boulder dropped in Taryn's gut. *We.*

Gemma. Gemma was the Sawtooth, or part of it. But how? The will to live spoke up in a loud protest inside Taryn, demanding she forget all of this, get across the river. Take that canoe. Survive. Live a long life and die an old lady. It surprised Taryn. She'd never before felt so strongly about living in a world without Gemma.

89

What if she could have Gemma back for good? Was that in the cards here in this wonderland of nightmares? And if so, could Taryn accept her in this form? As this creature? She'd said *in sickness and in health*, and she'd meant it. But this? This was a little extra.

Taryn squinted to see up the mountain to where the Sawtooth was sleeping. But it wasn't sleeping anymore. It stood, facing the river. That couldn't be Gemma, it wasn't possible. But why would Gemma lie? Her voice was real. But that monster was real too. Taryn's mind flipped and flopped like a fish on the shore. What if the Sawtooth was some type of mimic? A shapeshifter who lured victims by posing as their loved ones? What then?

It felt like the far side of the river was wooing her, crying for her to move toward life. A siren only Taryn could resist. She was tired and it wasn't just the exhaustion of being wounded. It was a quality of fatigue from living without Gemma, and now hearing her wife's audible voice again was life-giving. Moving away from her, across the river, felt like trying to pull a cart full of granite behind her.

"Prove you're really Gemma. That it's not just that monster trying to trick me."

"How?"

"The game. Do you remember—"

"James Joyce Carol Oates in the Water. Always ends in death."

Taryn cried out. Tears warmed her cheeks. It was really Gemma. She had come back. Taryn wanted out of the river and up that hill where she could hug her wife. Her body didn't respond though, didn't move a twitch toward it. Imagining coming back down the hill after crawling all the way up there felt impossible. *Was* impossible. Taryn had to show Gemma where she was.

But that was crazy, right? Taryn had seen what that monster did to Craig, heard its cries throughout the woods. Yet, this was Gemma, her wife. Surely, she was safe.

CHAPTER 18

"Gem," was all Taryn could push out in a breath.

"It's a lot to take in," Gemma replied. "Trust me, I know. But we really have to move faster. Sometimes they sleep for hours, but sometimes not. I haven't figured out their feeding rhythms yet, but they always pass out after a meal. It's like eating takes all their energy. That's why they tied that man up—"

"They were saving him for later," Taryn interrupted.

"Exactly. Mom's stirring, beginning to wake. She's always first, then Grandma, and then it happens fast, like dominoes. They all wake up from newest to oldest. When the last one finally wakes, she takes possession of the body. That's when it begins and I get a front-row seat to...murder. It's hell, babe."

"Why is this happening to you?" Taryn whispered.

"The ring. That's how the story goes, at least as it was passed from my grandma, to my mom, and then to me. Like some fucking oral tradition. There's a lot of details, a whole goddamn history in fact, but we don't have time to get into it. Long story short, anyone who wears that ring ends up here."

"Why can't you control the body?"

"The longer you're here, the more power you have. There are so many of them, I don't even know, like I said, at some point, they lose themselves like a drop of water lost in an ocean."

Pieces of a puzzle clicked into place for Taryn, and then calm came over her, unlike anything she'd felt since Gemma died.

"And when I die, I'll be the newest one since I've now worn the ring."

"What? No. No, that's not happening. You're giving me the ring and I'm going to destroy it. Put an end to all of this."

"How will you destroy a ring that survived the heat of cremation, Gem? A ring that might have survived for millennia?"

"Swallow it."

"What?" Taryn chuckled.

"It'll work. They want to protect the ring. It needs a wearer in order for us to be material in the world. No wearer and we can't exist. It's the only way to make sure another person doesn't find it and put it on. It wasn't until you put it on that I woke up here inside this creature."

"Why didn't you attack me right away?"

"Couldn't see you until you were cut and bleeding, and then we tracked you. When we finally came upon you, passed out on the trail, I realized it was you, wearing my old ring. The primordials didn't want you once they saw the ring. They pulled back and pursued the others instead, the biologists." Gemma sounded sad. Taryn's heart clenched. How could she ever live without Gemma again? Even if she was in this ghastly form. It was still her wife.

"But I thought you said they didn't want to hurt me because of the ring. So, I'm not in danger, right?"

"Babe, we have to get moving. Where are you?"

"I'm not showing myself until I get answers."

"But I can't protect you if they wake up."

"I understand the risk."

Gemma sighed. "After they killed the woman, they began discussing coming back for you, keeping you as a pet to ensure the ring always had a wearer."

"But I'd die eventually. Seems like a dumbass plan."

"They're strong; I didn't say they were smart. Being in my right mind and requiring way less sleep than them are my only real advantages. I can only operate the body when the rest are asleep. I went back for you while they were passed out. Put you in the den, knowing the wolf pups and the biologist were bloody enough for the primordials not to notice you for a while. It bought me a little time. But then you must have cleaned up because I can't see you anymore."

"Why not just take the ring then and there? Why put me in the den?"

"I wanted to help you get back to your camp. I was worried about your injury but didn't know how much time I had before the others woke up. Enough talk, baby. Where are you?"

"How will you swallow the ring? Once I take it off and give it to you, won't you disappear again? Doesn't the Sawtooth need a wearer for the ring?"

"Fuck," Gemma said, like she hadn't thought about that.

"You wore the ring all those years, and you were out here too, Gem. Why didn't you see the Sawtooth?"

"I did see it," Gemma whispered. "Why do you think I stressed over every small cut you got out here? The Sawtooth never hurt me, but I didn't understand why. Now I know it's because I was the wearer. Back then, I only knew that I could communicate with my mom, that she was somehow part of it. She didn't explain any of it to me. Every time I asked, she'd disappear. I stopped asking. I guess she assumed it was too late since I'd already worn the ring. Wanted me to live out my life without knowing what was coming."

"Well, that was a royal bust," Taryn said, anger seeping into her voice.

"You're still mad."

"I find it ironic that you were so eager to die, to avoid deterioration and now look at you. It's fucked up."

"Then you understand why I must have the ring. Destroy it. Find peace. It won't be long before I lose myself and become just like them. Help me."

"Help you? Help you leave me again? Is that what you're asking?" Taryn didn't bother to filter out the anger. Didn't care. Her mind was wonky and she wondered if perhaps it too was slipping, maybe she was growing hypothermic. The only thing that was clear, the only urge that mattered right then, was that she couldn't let Gemma go.

"No. I mean, yes. Help me get peace, and help me save you so you can live a long and happy life."

"You don't get it. You never got it. I don't want to be without you. You stole years away from me, like taking away the last drops of water in a desert. We had money. We could have made a home out here where you always wanted to live, forced that time to expand into something that mattered. Maybe you would have lived long enough for a treatment to show up. But you wouldn't hear of it, and just wanted to be done. You gave up on me. On us. I won't do the same."

"What are you talking about?" Panic laced Gemma's words.

Taryn didn't reply.

CHAPTER 19

"You have to fight," Taryn had said on the couch just a week before they were scheduled to fly overseas so Gemma could die. "You can't just give up."

Gemma had only smiled, reached across the couch for Taryn's hand. The same way she'd done over the months since her diagnosis. Gemma, who had somehow turned saintly through this process. Had become the perfect human, able to support Taryn in a way Taryn couldn't reciprocate. It only made Taryn angrier at herself. Laden with more guilt. But Taryn couldn't adjust her view. She couldn't accept Gemma's fate. Didn't believe she could survive without her wife. Taryn still had so much to give her.

Taryn hadn't wanted to look at Gemma, so she stared ahead, out their front window. At all their neighbors out shoveling the first snow, likely grumbling about the cold. All of them free of this heavy burden of death even though they were actually no more free of it than Gemma was. They too would face it one day. But probably not this week. Not next Monday, like Gemma. God, you never knew what the people around you were going through while you just lived your ho-hum life. Taryn watched the kids across the street push a snowball into the shape of a snowman's body. Just another day for everyone else.

"There's nothing to fight here," Gemma answered. "I would rather go while I remember myself, while I remember us."

"But the doctor said you might have years."

"We've discussed this so many times, Tare. Do you really think you'll change my mind at this point? Or that hearing me say it again will make things better for you? We're at a stalemate."

Taryn shrugged. Gemma was right. Taryn could hear this spiel an infinite number of times, but nothing would change her mind, her heart.

"The doctor also said that the disease could set in without warning," Gemma started. "I remember my mom's years. I don't want that for me. Or for you."

"What about what I want?"

This time she said it out loud. But Gemma only smiled and then winced gently, saintly, "It's not about what you want."

"But I'm the one who has to carry on without you."

"And you will. You'll fall in love again. I want that for you."

"It's not about what you want."

"Touché."

CHAPTER 20

It wasn't about what Gemma wanted. Not this time.

Taryn turned to face the far side of the river again. She moved slowly, so careful not to incur even a scrape. Nothing that would summon Gemma.

The thing was, it all made sense now.

If love was give and take, as they say, then marriage was a process of defining those terms. What was give and what was take? Taryn tried to give Gemma a reason to put off what the doctors called an "eventuality." Their love, memories they still had yet to make. But Gemma saw it as Taryn taking a choice from her.

Now, Gemma was trying to give Taryn an out. A way to *live*. But no, this was taking away Taryn's choice to have Gemma back again.

Who got to define the parameters of give and take? Taryn looked at the ring, now gleaming, washed by the river and glowing in the sunshine. Taryn and Gemma loved each other. Always had. Love was never the problem. It wasn't until their unspoken agreement—*being together is the most important thing*—had been shot to hell with Gemma's diagnosis and they'd been unable to re-evaluate. Unable to shift the terms of the agreement into something they could both live with.

She had accepted that Gemma would die young. But the terms of the agreement should be that Gemma go out in a blaze of glory, having sucked the breath out of the time they had left together. Because being together was the most important thing.

Gemma had refused. Tried to push another agreement on Taryn. A shitty agreement. That Taryn should sit idly by and watch Gemma abandon her. Watch her quit.

And now, this was Taryn's second chance to show Gemma that no, things weren't ideal. But they could make the most of it as long as they had each other. They would return to the old agreement and Taryn would give Gemma back the years that were stolen from her.

Taryn's vision blinked out for a beat while she crossed the river. The water numbed a line along her jaw. The sensation told her that she was still lucid, but panic flushed inside. Her vision returned, even though she was dizzy.

What had she just been thinking about? Something about the ring, and Gemma, and who got to decide the terms of the agreement.

Yes, that was right. Taryn had the ring in her possession whether Gemma liked it or not. This time it was Taryn's choice.

"Taryn?" Gemma said. "They're waking up. Please show me where you are. There's no more time."

Taryn reached arms out for dry shore, wind whipping cold on her fingers once out of the water. She was on the other side now and the canoe was only a bit further downriver. She could see it in the daylight.

"I'll show you where I am, but only if you help me into the canoe before I give you the ring. You'll have to bite it off my finger, you know that right? We're going to have to Gollum and Frodo in Mordor this shit. Or else you'll disappear when I take it off."

"I know," Gemma whispered, like she hated that part. Of course she did. Love was never the problem.

"Hurry, though," Gemma said. "Once the primordials are awake, I won't be able to help you and they won't swallow the ring."

Taryn crawled in the direction of the canoe until she found rope. She grabbed it, tugged a bit and all the slack tightened. The rope was attached to the bow of the canoe.

Taryn looked around for a sharp rock to cut herself with, but came across a stick instead. She made a slash across her cheek, imagined Gemma's finger caressing it, the way she always did after they made love. Saw Gemma's face in her mind, surrounded by light, turned toward her in their queen-size bed, the smell of coffee brewing on a lazy Saturday morning.

The Sawtooth was immediately before Taryn. A single, slate-colored hand outstretched, asking for the ring, while all the other arms hung limp. It was Gemma's hand. Taryn touched the palm, traced the lines, like she'd done so many times over the years with her wife's hand.

"Babe, please," Gemma pleaded.

"Put me in the canoe first, I can't get in by myself."

Another arm came to life and the creature lifted Taryn like she was a bag of groceries, set her into the heart of the canoe, then pushed it until the boat touched water. Gemma held on to the rope.

"It's time. They're almost here."

Taryn looked at the Sawtooth, her wife. It was repulsive and had nothing of her Gemma's features in it. But she could live with that. She had her own memories and pictures to remember her wife's beauty.

Taryn touched the ring, like Gemma used to do when she spun it. She could feel the Sawtooth's longing for it as the creature moved its enormous closed snout so near to Taryn's hand that she could feel hot breath. Poised to bite.

It pissed Taryn off all over again. That Gemma still wanted to get away more than she wanted to fight to be together. Find a way to make it work.

"Please live a long life," Gemma said in Taryn's mind. "Find love again. That's what I want for you." The Sawtooth's body twitched, reanimating. The mouth opened to show at least fifteen rows of jagged razorblade teeth. The breath was rank, smelled like the dead raccoon stuck under their deck in hundred-degree weather all those summers ago.

"Babe, this time, it doesn't matter what you want," Taryn said, and pulled the ring off her finger.

The Sawtooth tried to reach for Taryn, releasing the rope in the process, but the river pulled the canoe downstream. The monster came fully alive, arms and legs reeling as it tried to figure out what was happening. Then it let a cry loose. Taryn looked at the ring in her palm, clasped it and watched. The Sawtooth disappeared.

CHAPTER 21

Taryn needed to focus, stay alert, find the camp. Navigate this canoe so it didn't tip over, or float right by, miss its mark. Her mind was growing fuzzy again, like all of the energy she'd expended was drained out of her. She was jerking wildly with cold, but she put the ring inside her sports bra and gripped the plastic handle of the paddle. Slipping it into the water, she tried to keep the boat forward-facing.

She only had one job to do now. Keep the boat straight, and watch for signs of a basecamp. Seemed easy enough. Doable even for her wounded self.

Ahead, a curl of smoke wound through the sky. Likely the first campfire of the day, intended to boil water for coffee. Taryn screamed and placed the paddle in the water on the left side of the canoe to steer over to the right, where smoke was coming from.

"Help! Help me! I'm on the river!"

She had a few more yards until she'd reach—and then pass right by—the basecamp. The river was still gentle, but it created that white noise that could suck up any other sound. She kept yelling, crying, desperate to be heard. Her throat dry and gritty.

The smoke was closer now. What if she missed it? She pushed her arms to paddle faster, not allowing the current to pull her back out into the middle of the river. She was going too fast to bank the boat herself. Someone would need to wade out and catch it, reel her in.

That's when a man emerged from the woods, stood at the river's edge, a hand in a salute to shield his eyes from the early sun. He was about a hundred feet away. He waved at her, yelled something back into the woods and three more people joined him. They waded out into the river and laid hold of the canoe.

Gemma was right, this whole thing had to end. The Sawtooth, the madness, the killing. And Taryn would end it, would allow Gemma to dispose of the ring at some point. But not yet. Not while her wife still had so much life in her.

TWO MONTHS LATER

It was Taryn's first night in the new place. October was halfway gone, and she was settling in before the snow piled too high. The cabin wasn't perfect and would need some updating once winter was over. She wouldn't touch the floor-to-ceiling pine paneling in every room, but yes, the kitchen needed a new countertop and a fresh coat of paint on the cabinets. What color would Gemma like? She had never been one for decorating, but if Taryn thought about it hard enough, surely, she could come up with some options. Of course, she could always just *ask* Gemma too.

Taryn poured a cup of hot coffee and smiled to herself. She was happy—genuinely happy—for the first time in years. This felt right. Finally, she was living *Gemma's life*. Giving her wife this longtime dream of a home in the wilderness. She curled hands around the warm cup and walked over to the window, where the movers had set the couch after she told them she didn't know yet where it should go. It angled, facing the window like an enclosed seat. She shoved a box and a few piles of bedding aside so she could sit down. Gemma had always wanted a leather sofa, the sort that reclines. Taryn thought they were ugly and cold. But it turned out that it was nothing a thick sweater and tights couldn't solve. Lots of blankets. She turned her face to smell the leather and her stomach flipped when she imagined Gemma's surprise, delight even, that she'd caved and bought a leather couch for Gemma's dream home.

This place would work fine. Not like there were a lot of options out here, and she'd been watching the listings online from day one, even in the hospital. Put the house in Boise up for sale right away too. It seemed like end of summer might be a good time to buy in the mountains.

Sellers would be eager to avoid another winter maintaining a second property they only use three months out of the year, and buyers wouldn't be thinking about summer properties until at least March. When she found this one and it was situated perfectly with a long driveway connecting up to the main road, she had a good feeling about it. It had running water, a septic system, and best of all—internet. She'd set her heart on making an offer even before she tapped through the gallery of images on her phone. If it had the structural stuff in place, cosmetic changes to the inside were just details. Plus, it'd give her something to do. Once the sale was final, and she was walking around again, she bought a snowmobile and a trailer, along with a vehicle that could tow it. Nobody said it'd be cheap to make this life work, but the home in Boise had fetched a good price and she paid cash for the cabin. With internet out there, she could work on a freelance basis when she felt like it. If money got too low. If she even cared about money by that point.

But the bottom line was that Taryn had done it, and it was perfect. A cozy cabin burrowed into the woods, near the river. The Sawtooth Mountains climbed up behind the place, stretching into those toothy, treeless peaks. The nearest town was Gemma's Garden Valley, so Taryn could drive there in an afternoon for groceries, but far enough out that she—*they*—could be alone.

Surrounded by boxes, Taryn had sent the movers off with a huge tip for their trouble in coming all the way out there. The daylight was receding even though it was only slightly past dinnertime. October had brought shorter days, longer nights. Fine with Taryn. Days, nights, none of that mattered anymore.

She peered out the window and watched the river move slowly below until it was wrapped in golden sunset, threatening to vanish at any moment.

Taryn pulled on boots and wrapped a blanket around her shoulders. She picked up a box from its spot on a cardboard stack next to the door. She gripped it tightly. It was so small that her cage of fingers almost hid it. With her other hand, she reached for the safety pin tucked away in her pocket. Walking out onto the small stoop of steps, she breathed in the fresh air and caught the scent of wet leaves, a bit of pine too. She'd never felt so alive, it was almost electric. Gemma had been right all along. This was the better way to live.

Taryn pulled the golden ring out of the box and slipped it on her finger for the first time since that day she almost died in the mountains. The last time she spoke with Gemma. She opened the pin and pricked her index finger. A single drop of blood ballooned on the tip.

Just as the last hints of light were drawing down, giving in to darkness, Taryn heard something.

A cry that rang out so loud, she had to cover her ears. But before she did that, she heard one voice lifted above the chorus of thousands. Gemma's voice. She would be here any minute.

END

ACKNOWLEDGEMENTS

Thank you to everyone who has helped me on the path to publishing *Sawtooth*. There are too many to name, but I want to call out a few.

First, my husband, Chris, to whom I've dedicated the book. He's an avid outdoorsman and the one who gave me the idea for what became *Sawtooth*. I wanted to think up something that might actually scare him when he's in the woods alone because I'm mean like that. Also, he is one of three people who have the most skin in the game of my budding writing career. He's the first to celebrate my successes, and the first to make the sacrifices it takes to give me time and space to write. Thank you, Chris, for carrying so much of our family and home life so that I can reach for this dream. I'm so grateful for you and lucky to have you.

The other two with skin in the game, are my kids, Cameron and Jonathan. Eternal thanks to you two for cheering me on. So proud to be your mom.

Thanks to Sadie Hartmann who read the first draft of this book and gave me absolutely invaluable feedback that I was able to use. Thanks, Sadie, for your continued support, and for everything you do for horror fiction. I'm lucky to know you!

Thank you to all the badass Bookstagrammers, Booktokers, and Booktubers for reading my stuff and sharing your experiences with it. I know what you do is a labor of love, but the time and dedication it takes to continually promote horror and thriller books is admirable, and I'm very thankful for you all. You're the unsung heroes of horror fiction—especially indie fiction!

Thanks to Noelle Ihli, Anna Gamel, Kelsey Zedwick, and Jeanne Allen, who are about the best beta readers a girl could ask for. Each of you asked fantastic skeptical questions, pointed out plot holes, and generally made suggestions that strengthened the story.

Thanks to my sister-in-law, Julie Dresback, for our hiking adventures in the Sawtooth Mountains, and many more to come.

Thanks to Luke Spooner for a mind-blowing cover. You're so talented and I hope to work with you again in the future.

Thank you, Joe Sullivan, for taking a chance on this story and helping bring it to life in the world. I've loved working with you, and Cemetery Gates has been a dream press for me. I'm so grateful that you said yes!

Lastly, thank you reader. There are so many great books to choose from, and most of us only have a few hours of free time in a day, if that. I'm honored and humbled that you chose to spend your time reading *Sawtooth*.

AUTHOR'S NOTE

Hey you!

Thanks so much for picking up *Sawtooth*. If you liked this story, a positive review would mean so much to me. Honest reviews help other readers decide if the book is for them or not, and indie authors like me rely heavily on word-of-mouth recommendations. Trust me, your two-sentence review matters.

Again, thank you for reading. xo

A lifelong PNW girl, Steph is from Spokane, Washington, but currently lives in Boise, Idaho, with her husband and their two teens. Her short fiction appears in *Dark Matter Presents: Human Monsters* and *Mother: Tales of Love and Terror.* Both are Bram Stoker-nominated anthologies. Her debut novel, *The Vein,* is available through Dark Matter INK, and her next horror novel, *The Threshing Floor*, is forthcoming in November 2024, also through INK. *Sawtooth* is her first novella. When Steph's not working on her next story, she's devouring horror, thriller, and even romance books. Or taxiing her teens around town for their sports and social lives. Find her on Instagram/Threads @stephnelsonauthor, and on Twitter/X @stephdresnelson.